SHOTGUN

ED McBAIN

SHOTGUN

An 87th Precinct Mystery

UNABRIDGED

PAN BOOKS LTD : LONDON

First published in Great Britain 1969 by
Hamish Hamilton Ltd.
This edition published 1971 by Pan Books Ltd,
33 Tothill Street, London, S.W.1

ISBN 0 330 02702 6

*Printed and bound in England by
Hazell Watson & Viney Ltd,
Aylesbury, Bucks*

This is for
Corinne and Ken Davis

ONE

DETECTIVE BERT KLING went outside to throw up.

Coming down the corridor towards him, Detective Steve Carella saw the look on his face, said, 'What's the matter, kid?' as he brushed past, and then understood immediately. He hesitated before approaching the patrolman stationed outside the apartment door. Then, with a brief nod of resignation, he took his shield from where it was pinned inside his wallet, fastened it to the pocket of his suit jacket, exchanged only the shortest glance with the patrolman, and entered the apartment.

The building was on South Engels in an upper middle-class area on the northern fringe of the 87th Precinct, not a part of Smoke Rise, nor even in that section of buildings lining the River Harb, but farther east and somewhat less fashionable than either. The patrolman had been stationed outside the apartment's service entrance, so that was where Carella went in. He found himself in a smallish kitchen with an abundance of tile, a spotlessly clean chequerboard vinyl floor, an equally clean, white enamel-top table, and appliances that noisily hummed with age.

The first body was in the living-room.

The woman, as the newspapers would faithfully report later, was clad only in nylon panties, but there was not the faintest suggestion of sexuality about her; the image such a description evoked was entirely invalid because the woman was dead, the woman was sprawled in an utterly grotesque posture of lifelessness, her face and part of her skull ripped away by what appeared even at first glance to have been a shotgun blast. She was a woman in her late thirties perhaps, possibly attractive when alive, seeming now only a loose bundle of bones held together by a flaccid skin case. She had soiled herself in death, either in fear before the act, or in a relaxation of sphincter muscles when the shotgun blast tore away half her head. She was wearing a wedding band on her left hand, no engagement ring. She was lying exposed in front of a large sofa slip-covered in a riotous print of hibiscus blooms. Two spent shotgun-cartridge cases were on the rug beside her. Her blood had soaked into the pale-blue tufts of the rug and spread in a wide puddle beneath her head. It was this scene that had sent Bert Kling rushing out of the apartment.

Steve Carella had a stronger stomach, or perhaps he was simply a more experienced cop. He left the living-room and proceeded into the apartment's master bedroom.

A man in undershorts and undershirt was lying just inside the door in an almost foetal position. His entire face and most of his head had been blown away. His thumb was locked around the trigger of the shotgun still clutched in one hand; the barrel of the 12-gauge gun lay close to what remained of his jaw. A single spent cartridge case was on the floor beside his open head, surrounded by several small white objects. It took Carella a moment to realize they were fragmented teeth.

He went outside.

Monoghan and Monroe, the two bulls on mandatory call from Homicide, were standing in the hallway.

'Nice one, huh?' Monoghan said.

'Beauty,' Monroe said.

'Takes all kinds,' Monoghan said.

'More nuts outside than in,' Monroe said.

They had played this particular scene before. Nothing fazed them; they had seen it all and heard it all. They stood in stoic nonchalance against the buff-coloured wall of the building's hallway, both smoking cigars, both dressed in black topcoats and grey fedoras, the Tweedledum and Tweedledee of criminal detection. A window at the far end of the hallway, newly washed because this was Saturday and yesterday was when the cleaning service had come to do the building, was open a trifle at the bottom. A brisk October breeze swept the corridor, fresh and clean and reeking of life. Beyond the window, the early-morning sun limned the city's towers. A haze hung in the distant sky.

'Think the guy went berserk?' Monroe asked Carella.

'Sure,' Monoghan said. 'Plugged his wife and then went into the bedroom to give himself the *coup d'état*.'

'*De grâce*,' Monroe corrected.

'Sure,' Monoghan said, and shrugged.

Carella said nothing.

'Do us a favour,' Monroe said to Carella.

'Save us a lot of paperwork.'

'Don't make this a big deal.'

'It's pure and simple. He knocked her off, and then turned the gun on himself.'

'Don't make it a federal case.'

'I wonder who heard the shots,' Carella said.

'Huh?'

'It must have happened last night sometime. I wonder who heard the shots.'

'In prime time, nobody hears shots,' Monroe said.

'I also wonder who called it in. Was Kling here when you arrived?'

'The blond cop?'

'Yes.'

'He was here,' Monroe said.

'A little pale around the gills, but here,' Monoghan said.

'Did he say how he got the squeal?'

'Milkman called him,' Monoghan said.

'The milkman?'

'Yeah.'

'How come?'

'Saw the door open, thought it was strange.'

'What door?'

'To the kitchen. The service entrance.'

'It was open?'

'*Wide* open.'

'What time was this?'

'I don't know. An hour or so ago.' Monoghan looked at his watch. 'About five o'clock, I guess.'

'The kitchen door was *open* at five o'clock in the morning?'

'That's what the milkman said. Ask Kling, he took a statement.'

'One thing I hate,' Monroe said, 'is these early morning calls.'

'Anyway, this one looks about wrapped up,' Monoghan said. He met Carella's eyes. 'Right, Carella?'

'You think so?'

'I could draw you a blueprint and write the whole scenario,' Monoghan said.

'Gee, I wish you would,' Carella said. 'Save us a whole lot of time.'

'Only trouble is,' Monoghan said, 'a homicide belongs to the precinct taking the squeal.'

'Yeah, that's a shame,' Monroe said.

'So I guess we'll have to leave it to you fellows, after all.'

'I guess so.'

Monroe took out a handkerchief, blew his nose, put the handkerchief back into his pocket and then said, 'Carella, let's close it as soon as possible, huh?'

'Why?'

'Because it's an obvious goddamn case, that's why.'

'Except for the door being wide open at five in the morning.'

'A technicality,' Monroe said.

'You start looking around, you'll probably find a note the old man left.'

'You think so, huh?' Carella said.

'Sure, they usually leave notes. It's because they're filled with remorse ...'

'Regret,' Monroe said.

'So they write a note begging the world to understand they're really only nice guys who just happened to behave bad once in their lives. A slight lapse, you know what I mean?'

10

'A minor little bit of mischief.'

'Please understand.'

'Please forgive.'

'That's why they leave notes.'

'You're sure to find one,' Monroe said. 'You just look around, you'll find one.'

'You think it'll tell us about that spent cartridge case?' Carella asked.

'Huh?' Monroe said.

'The one in the bedroom alongside the dead man.'

'What about it?'

'He's holding a 12-gauge *pump* shotgun,' Carella said.

'Yeah?'

'That means you've got to pump it to eject the spent cartridge and get the next one into the firing chamber. Maybe you'd like to tell me how he managed to shoot himself in the head and then pump the gun to eject that cartridge.'

'Boy,' Monroe said.

The milkman was still in a state of shock. He and Kling made a perfect couple, each sitting pale and trembling across from Carella in the small luncheonette several blocks from the apartment building. It was 6.10 AM and the place had just opened. Several truck drivers were sitting at the counter, sharing a privileged early-morning jocularity with the owner of the place. A sleepy-eyed waitress wearing a uniform already soiled, swivelled over to the leatherette booth where Carella and his wan companions sat, and took their breakfast orders. Both Kling and the milkman ordered only coffee.

'What time did you discover the open door, Mr Novello?' Carella asked the milkman.

'About a quarter to five. Just before I called the police. What time was that?' he asked Kling.

'Murchison clocked the squeal in at four forty-seven,' Kling said.

'Is that when you usually deliver milk in that building?'

'Yeah, I start there about four-thirty. I'm generally out

11

by five. I start on the top floor, you know, and work my way down. The Leydens live on the third floor.'

'All right, what happened?'

'I already told your partner.'

'Let's hear it again.'

'Well, I come to the back door, which is where I usually make my delivery – they got a milk catch on the door, you know what I mean?'

'Yes,' Carella said.

'It's this wire thing,' Novello said, explaining anyway, 'that has a loop goes around the neck of the bottle. You put the bottle in it, then you shove the catch back through this hole in the door, and it drops down on the inside, locking the bottle in, you know what I mean?'

'Yes,' Carella said again.

'They take a bottle every other morning, the Leydens. You find with most people in the neighbourhood, they just take enough to get them through breakfast, you see, and later they shop at the grocery for however much more they'll need. That's the way it works.'

'I see. Go on.'

'So I come down to the third floor . . .'

'How?'

'Huh? Oh, by the steps. I walked down from the fourth floor. I got Levine and Davidson on the fourth floor, and then only the Leydens on three. By the steps.'

'Yes?'

'And I put down the carrier, and I'm reaching for the bottle when I see the kitchen door is open.'

'*Wide* open or just ajar?'

'Wide open. I could see right in the kitchen and also some of the living-room.'

'So what'd you do?'

'I didn't know what to do. I figured maybe I should just close the door and beat it, you know? But then I wondered what the kitchen door was doing open at five o'clock in the morning. I mean, what's the *door* doing open?'

'Did you go in?'

12

'I went in.'

'And saw the bodies?'

'I saw only Mrs Leyden,' Novello said, and swallowed.

'Then what did you do?'

'I went downstairs and called the police.'

'Why didn't you use the phone in the apartment?'

'I didn't want to get my fingerprints on nothing. I didn't touch nothing in that apartment, I didn't want to get involved in nothing.'

'Where'd you make your call from?'

'There's an all-night cafeteria on Dixon, I called from there.'

'Then what?'

'I was told to go back to the building and wait, which is what I did. That's when Mr Kling here come over to investigate.'

'Did you call your boss?'

'Yeah, right after I hung up with Mr Kling. I'm a working man, you know, I still had milk to deliver.' Novello sighed and said, 'He sent out another man to finish the route. I sure hope he don't dock me for it.'

'You did the right thing, Mr Novello,' Carella said.

'I hope so. It's a tough decision to make, you know? Like your first instinct is to just get out of there, just get as far away as possible. It's a funny thing. It scares you. A thing like that.'

'But you called the police.'

'Yeah, well . . .' Novello shrugged. 'I liked that lady. She was a nice lady. She used to give me a cup of coffee every Wednesday when I come around to collect the bill. What the hell, she didn't have to do that.' He shook his head. 'I can't understand it. I met Mr Leyden one Wednesday when he was home, he travels a lot, you know, I think he sells heavy machinery or something. He seemed like a very nice man. He was telling me about how he loved his job and all, you know, but how he didn't like being away from home for such long periods of time, poor guy was sometimes on

13

the road two or three months at a stretch. He seemed like a really nice man.'

'When was this?'

'Oh, I don't know, during the summer sometime.'

'Was that the only time you'd seen them together?'

'Yeah, just that once. But they seemed like a real happy couple, you know what I mean? You know, you can tell when a man and his wife ain't getting along. But she kept calling him "honey" and "dearie" and things like that, you could see they were happy. I don't want to sound corny, but you could see they ...' Novello paused. 'Loved each other,' he said at last.

'Now, you say you went into the building at four-fifteen, is that right, Mr Novello?'

'No, four-thirty,' Novello said. 'That's the time I usually go in, about four-thirty.'

'And went directly to the tenth floor?'

'Yeah. There's a self-service elevator, you know, so I just take that up each morning.'

'See anyone in the lobby?'

'Not a soul.'

'Anyone stirring in the building?'

'Just Mr Jacobson, he's a postman.'

'Where'd you see him?'

'On the fifth floor. He usually leaves about a quarter to five each morning, he works all the way up in River-head. He probably stops for breakfast, you know, and then goes to work. They got to be in early, those letter carriers.'

'He say anything to you?'

'Yeah,' he said, "Good morning, Jimmy", and I said, "Good morning, Mr Jacobson, little chilly out there this morning". Something like that. We usually exchange a few words, you know. They been taking milk from me for seven years now, the Jacobsons. We whisper, you know, because the whole building's usually asleep.'

'See anybody else?'

'Not a soul.'

14

'Either before or after you discovered Mrs Leyden's body?'

'Just Mr Jacobson, nobody else.'

'Okay, Mr Novello, thanks very much,' Carella said. 'Bert? You have anything to ask?'

'No, nothing,' Kling said. He was still pale. He had hardly touched his coffee.

'Why don't you take a break, meet me at the building later?' Carella suggested.

'No, I'll stick with it,' Kling said.

'It scares you, you know?' Novello said. 'A thing like that.'

TWO

BECAUSE TAKING the fingerprints of a suicide or homicide victim is mandatory, someone inherited the pleasant task of holding hands with two separate corpses that Saturday morning.

The someone was a laboratory technician named Detective 3rd/Grade Marshall Davies. He was a new technician, and he generally got the crummy jobs like picking glass headlight slivers out of a dead accident victim's back, or vacuuming the clothes of a man who'd been hit seven times with a hatchet, or – like now – fingerprinting corpses.

Fresh dead bodies are easier to fingerprint than those that have been around awhile. That's one of the small consolations in this racket, Davies thought as he worked, the knowledge that all you have to do with a fresh dead body, where the fingers haven't yet clenched up, is apply the ink directly to each separate finger, *comme ça!* (he applied the ink to Rose Leyden's extended forefinger, using a small roller), and then take your impression with paper attached to a spoon-shaped piece of wood, *voilà*, he thought, stop it, you're not even French. Nine fingers to go on the lady, he thought, or, to be precise, *seven* fingers and two thumbs. We then administer to the gentleman in his undershorts in the bedroom, some job. My mother said I should become an accountant, but I said, No, Mama, police work is exciting. So here's Saturday morning, and Detective 3rd/Grade Marshall Davies is taking fingerprints from dead people, instead of playing ball in the park with his three-year-old son. Come on, lady, give me your ring finger.

He studied the ring on the third finger of her left hand. It was an ornately carved gold wedding band, very pretty, it would go into the estate of Rose Leyden, some relative would claim it, together with all her other worldly possessions, what a goddamn waste death was.

'How we doing there?' a voice behind him asked.

Detective 3rd/Grade Marshall Davies, Police Laboratory, looked up and over his shoulder into the face of Detective 3rd/Grade Richard Genero, 87th Squad. Genero was a new detective, too, having been promoted from patrolman only this past April after cracking a case in which two young hoodlums were running around setting fire to drunken vagrants. He was the youngest detective on the squad, and the greenest, and so he got all the lousy jobs nobody else wanted, like hanging around an apartment and watching new laboratory technicians fingerprint corpses.

'Oh, so-so,' Davies said, thinking he did not need conversation with a flatfoot, not while he was busy with such gruesome work.

'What's that thing there?' Genero asked.

Davies looked at him.

'*There*,' Genero said, as though repetition would make his question more meaningful.

'It's a semilunar-shaped piece of wood,' Davies replied, and sighed.

'What's it used for?'

Davies, who considered himself something of a wit, looked at Genero again, and then said, 'Can't you see I'm giving the lady a manicure?'

'Huh?' Genero said.

'Sure. I use this piece of wood to hold each finger while I paint her nails. What'd you think I used it for?'

'Gee, I don't know,' Genero, who was something of a wit himself, replied. 'I thought it was a wooden thermometer you were planning to shove up your ass.'

The two new detectives glared at each other.

'Buzz off,' Davies said flatly.

'My pleasure,' Genero said, and walked off steaming.

Goddamn flatfoot, Davies thought, got nothing to do but bother a man trying to do a day's work. Diligently, he inked each of Rose Leyden's fingers and thumbs, making his im-

17

pressions, keeping the slips of paper separated and in sequence so that he could later mark each one according to finger. He sometimes wondered why the police bothered with fingerprints at all, especially in a case like this where it was obvious that the dead people were decent citizens living in a good neighbourhood. Neither of them would have a police record, of course, and unless the guy had been in the armed forces at one time or another, his fingerprints would not be in the FBI files either. So what was the point? Did anyone ever stop to realize how many people in the United States, especially women, had never in their lives been fingerprinted? Of course not. This whole thing about fingerprints was something invented by the police in order to scare not criminals but civilians. The criminal doing a job knew that his prints already were on file someplace, or would be one day, so he wore gloves as a matter of course. The civilian committing a crime usually acted in the heat of passion, and when it's hot you don't wear gloves. But the civilian cracks under pressure more easily than the habitual criminal does, especially if the cops come out suddenly with a statement like, 'And the fingerprints on the gun happen to match the fingerprints we found on your toothbrush in the bathroom, ah-*ha*, got you!' All bullshit, Davies thought, and continued fingerprinting a dead lady who, like most other ladies in America, dead or alive, had probably never had her prints taken before. It's a shame the honour had to wait till now, Davies thought, when you're laying stone-cold dead in your own living-room, missing all of your face and part of your head, and soaked with blood and whatever other corruption, Jesus, I'll be sick in a minute, Davies thought.

Do the job, he thought.

Stop thinking.

He stopped thinking, and he did the job.

The jewellery was spread on top of Carella's desk, and the woman sitting opposite him studied it with a careful eye but said nothing.

18

Her name was Mrs Gloria Leyden, and she was the widowed mother of Andrew Leyden, and she sat in corseted disbelief in the squad room and looked at the jewellery and refused to commit herself because committing herself would be the same thing as acknowledging that her son was dead.

'Well?' Carella said.

'Well, what?' she answered. She was a red-faced woman with a pug nose and puffy cheeks. Her hair was a violet-white, neatly coiffed, her bosom as ample as a pouter pigeon's, her eyes small and sharp and blue behind harlequin spectacles.

'Do you recognize any of this jewellery?'

'Why is it important that I recognize any of it?' Mrs Leyden asked.

'Well,' Carella said, 'we try to make a positive identification wherever possible. In a case like this, where the bodies . . .'

'It's hard to tell anything from jewellery,' Mrs Leyden said.

'Well, take this ring for example, it's from the University of Wisconsin, and there's a date inside it, June 1950, and also the engraved initials A.L.L. It was found on the right ring finger of the dead man, and I'm asking you now if you recognize it.'

'There are a lot of rings from the University of Wisconsin,' Mrs Leyden said.

'Did your son go to the University of Wisconsin?'

'Yes.'

'When was he graduated?'

'In June of 1950.'

'And his name is Andrew Leyden?'

'Yes.'

'What's his middle name?'

'Lloyd.'

'Then the initials in this ring, A.L.L., *could* be your son's initials.'

'There are lots of people with the initials A.L.L.'

19

'Yes,' Carella said. 'Well, how about this other ring, Mrs Leyden? It was found on the man's third finger left hand, and it's obviously a wedding band. The woman was wearing the same ring, narrower and smaller of course, but the same design. Do you recognize this ring?'

'Who looks at rings?' Mrs Leyden said.

'Well, it's very nicely carved, and it's an unusual wedding band, so perhaps you would have noticed if your son and daughter-in-law ever wore wedding bands similar to it.'

'Similar?'

'*Identical* to it,' Carella amended. 'The other wedding band there was taken from the woman's hand.' He pointed at it with a pencil.

'All wedding rings look alike to me,' Mrs Leyden said.

'This locket was around the dead woman's neck,' Carella said. He lifted the locket, a gold heart on a slender gold chain. 'There are two pictures in it,' he said, and opened the locket. 'Do you recognize either of these people in the pictures?'

'Yes,' Mrs Leyden said.

'Who are they?'

'The man is my son. The woman is my daughter-in-law.' Mrs Leyden nodded. 'That doesn't mean either of them is dead,' she said.

'Mrs Leyden . . .'

'I want to see the bodies.'

'They're at the mortuary. I don't think seeing the bodies is going to . . .'

'I want to see them. You're telling me my son is dead, and you're asking me to say, *Yes*, that's his college ring. *Yes*, that's his wedding ring. *Yes*, that's his picture in the locket there, you're asking me to say he's *dead!*'

'That's right, Mrs Leyden.'

'Show me his body,' Mrs Leyden said. 'Then I'll tell you if he's dead or not.'

'Both victims were shot at close range with a shotgun,' Carella said. 'In the face.'

'Yes, you've already told me that.'

'Mrs Leyden, a 12-gauge shotgun fired at close range doesn't leave much ...'

'I want to see the bodies,' Mrs Leyden said.

'Okay,' Carella said, and sighed, and called downstairs for a car.

A hospital mortuary is never a cheerful place, but it is perhaps least cheerful on a Saturday afternoon. The weekend is not a good time for dying, you should never die any time between Friday evening and Monday morning. Wednesday is the best day for dying except in some towns in Connecticut where even the barber shops are closed on Wednesday. But as a general rule, if you're going to die, Wednesday is a nice day for it. This was Saturday, and a lot of people had inconsiderately and with absolutely no regard for the calendar died in the hospital that morning and had been taken downstairs to be put on ice. In addition, through assorted accidents and acts of violence, a lot of other people had died elsewhere in the city and had been transported to the hospital for autopsy and what-have-you; so the mortuary attendant had been very busy, and he didn't need a cop coming around at 2 PM with a fat lady in a corset right when he was in the middle of reading a dirty book. The dirty book was a very good one, he was up to the part where they were whipping the girl and telling her she must never raise her eyes and must obey them and be ready at all times, it was a very good book.

'Leyden,' Carella said to the attendant, 'Andrew and Rose.'

'We got no Leydens here,' the attendant said, 'neither Andrew *nor* Rose.'

'They came in some time this morning,' Carella said.

'I been here since eight o'clock this morning, and there ain't no Leydens,' the attendant said.

'Well, check your list there,' Carella said.

'I looked at the list when I come on.'

'Well, look at it again.'

'I know every name on this list.'

'Pal ...' Carella started.

'Okay, okay,' the attendant said, and put down his book, and studied the list and said, 'Leyden, Andrew and Rose, is that it?'

'That's it.'

'I musta missed them when I checked the list earlier.'

'Yeah, you *must* have.'

'Which one you want to see?'

'Both,' Carella said.

'They're not together. I got the woman over here and the man over there.'

'Well, let's see the woman first,' Carella said.

'Suit yourself, six of one, half a dozen of the other,' the attendant said, and rose, and led them across the room. The room was large and echoing, lighted with fluorescent, stinking of antiseptic. The name LEYDEN, ROSE was lettered in pencil on a cardboard tag that had been slipped into a holder on the small door set in a row of identical small doors. There was a handle on the door. The attendant grabbed the handle and opened the door, and a rush of cold air touched Carella's face like a breath from the grave, and then the metal drawer came out a trifle on its ballbearing rollers, and they looked down at the shattered head and missing face of the person they presumed was Rose Leyden. The attendant rolled the drawer out farther, showing the woman's naked body, the bloodstains still on her neck and breasts and belly. Beside him, Mrs Gloria Leyden gasped and turned away.

'Is it your daughter-in-law?' Carella asked.

'Yes,' Mrs Leyden said.

'How do you know?'

'The beauty spot.'

'Which beauty spot, ma'am?'

'On her ... just above her breast. She ... my son thought it was very attractive ... it ... you could see it whenever Rose wore anything low cut ... it ... that's my daughter-in-law. That's Rose.'

Carella nodded to the attendant, who rolled the drawer

back into the refrigerator compartment, and then closed the door.

'Want to see the man?' he asked.

'Mrs Leyden?'

'I don't think I could bear it.'

'Then, Mrs Leyden, can you tell me if your son had any scars or tattoos? Any visible markings on his body that ...'

'What?' Mrs Leyden said.

'Any scars or ...'

'Yes, he had a tattoo.'

'Where would that be, Mrs Leyden?'

'What? I'm sorry, what did you say?'

'The tattoo. Where? ...'

'His arm. It was on his arm.'

'What sort of a tattoo?'

'A very simple one. He had it done when he was a boy. He must have been seventeen or eighteen. He'd been rejected by the service, you see, he had a punctured eardrum and ... and I guess he wanted to feel grown-up and ... manly. So he had himself tattooed.'

'And what does the tattoo look like, Mrs Leyden?'

'It's a dagger. A dagger in blue outline. And across it, in red, is his name, Andy.'

'I see,' Carella said. 'Would you ... Mrs Leyden, would you mind waiting here a moment, please?'

'Are you going to look to see if he ... if the ... if the man has a tattoo?'

'Yes.'

'It's his left arm,' Mrs Leyden said, and turned away.

Carella followed the attendant across the room to where the male corpses were stacked in their refrigerated compartments. 'Leyden, Leyden, Leyden,' the attendant said, 'here we are, Leyden,' and opened one of the doors and pulled out the drawer. The faceless dead man had a blue dagger, two inches long, tattooed on his left arm. The single word 'Andy', in red letters, ran horizontally across the blade of the dagger.

'Okay,' Carella said.

23

The attendant slid back the drawer. Carella walked across the room to where Mrs Leyden was standing. She looked up at him.

'It's your son,' he said.

Mrs Leyden nodded and said nothing.

They began walking towards the exit door together. Carella was a tall man wearing a brown business suit, his hair brown, his eyes brown, a pained expression sitting on them now as he walked beside the small corseted lady with the large sloping bosom and the ridiculous violet-white hair, a ludicrous couple with nothing more in common than death. At the door, she stopped, and put her hand on Carella's arm and looked up into his face, and very softly said, 'I think I *will* have to see him'.

'Mrs Leyden . . .'

'Because if I don't . . . if I don't look at him and see for myself . . . I'll never believe he's dead. I don't think I could bear going through life hoping he'll suddenly turn the next corner.'

They went back across the room, their heels clicking on the vinyl-tiled floor. The attendant rolled out the drawer and Mrs Leyden looked into the open red and gaping hole in the head of the corpse that lay stiff and cold on the cold aluminium rack, and then the attendant pulled the drawer farther out, and she looked at the corpse's arm silently, and then reached out as though to trace the outline of the blue dagger with its red letters, but stopped her hand in mid-motion instead, and covered her face and said, 'Yes, it's my son, yes,' and began weeping.

There were wild prints in the apartment.

Most of the prints, as expected, belonged to the dead man and his wife, but there were other prints as well, wild prints that belonged to neither of them.

The wild prints had been left by someone with very large hands, presumably a man, but possibly a woman. The wild prints were on doorknobs and doorjambs, the wild prints were on a glass in the kitchen, the wild prints were on a

24

dresser top. But most important, the wild prints were all over the shotgun. The third party who had been in that apartment on the night the Leydens were killed had roamed the place at will, gloveless, touching things freely and with apparent immunity, feeling confident enough to have left perfectly clear latent impressions on the shotgun stock and barrel, and a portion of a print on the trigger itself

The laboratory technicians were jubilant.

They sent their prints to the Bureau of Criminal Identification, the ones they had lifted from Rose and Andrew Leyden, and the ones they had discovered all over the apartment, the wild prints belonging to the big-handed man or woman who had possibly committed the murders. The BCI reported back late that afternoon, stating that they had no record for either Rose or Andrew Leyden, which was not surprising since neither of the pair had ever been arrested in their lives.

The case could have been solved that very afternoon if the BCI had come up with a make on the wild prints.

They didn't.

THREE

IT WAS a good October.

October is the best month anyway, but this October was a rare one. There had been only one rainy day at the very beginning of the month, and clear blue skies from then on, the breezes carrying just enough bite to make topcoats necessary, but never menacing, never threatening winter itself, even though it was just around the corner.

Carella had read somewhere that this city was the second sunniest city in America, Los Angeles being the first, and today he was ready to believe it. Miami had doubtless taken a fit, not to mention Palm Springs and perhaps Fresno, but there it was in black and white in a national magazine, *this* city was the second sunniest city in the United States, meaning that even when it was cold enough here to freeze you to the pavement, the sun was nonetheless shining.

The sun was shining brightly that Monday morning, October 28th, when he and Bert Kling left the squad room to head downtown. Kling was coatless and hatless, his blond hair gently stirring in the breeze that came in off the river to the north. Carella was wearing a tan trenchcoat and feeling like a private eye. Both men came down the station steps swiftly, Kling as tall as Carella, but broader and heavier, each walking with a brisk athletic stride, pausing on the sidewalk to look up at the magnificent blue sky, and grinning, and then walking swiftly and energetically and vigorously to where Kling had parked his car up the street.

'God, what a day!' he said. 'Days like this, I feel like sleeping till noon and then going to the park and sleeping some more.'

'Yeah, it's a beauty,' Carella said.

26

Kling started the car. Carella opened the window on his side and breathed deeply, and smiled.

They drove downtown with no sense of urgency. The sun was dazzling on the River Harb, the cliffs on the farther shore rising in sheer magnificence against a flawless blue expanse of sky. A red and green tugboat lazed its way upstream, a foghorn bleated, a single gull dipped in grey and white arcs over the filigreed water. The men discussed business only once on the way downtown, and that was when Kling asked whether the FBI had got back to them yet on the prints found in the Leyden apartment. Carella said, No, they hadn't, and then both men put the case out of mind again.

American Tractor & Machine was located on Bixby, two blocks west of Remington Circle. It was on the tenth floor of a steel and glass structure that reflected sky and sun in a dizzying multi-windowed whirl, making the building itself seem alive. An elevator whisked them aloft, polished aluminium doors opened soundlessly, and they found themselves in a lushly carpeted reception room, the AT & M logo prominently displayed behind a sleek walnut desk at which sat a pretty blonde receptionist wearing a miniskirt. The impression was hardly one of heavy machinery. The girl was petite, perhaps nineteen, with china-blue eyes that she batted first at Carella and then at Kling after seeing the wedding band on Carella's hand.

'We're detectives,' Carella said, and showed her the potsy. 'We'd like to talk to Andrew Leyden's superior.'

'Oh yes, isn't it terrible?' the girl said.

'Yes,' Carella said.

'*Isn't* it?' she said to Kling, and batted her blue eyes again, the lashes incredibly long and probably fake, Carella thought.

'Yes,' Kling said. 'Did you know Mr Leyden?'

'Oh, yes, certainly,' the girl said, and then said, 'Does that make me a suspect?'

'No, not necessarily,' Kling said, and smiled.

'I thought you might be going to investigate me or something,' the girl said, and then laughed, striving for a throaty undertone which she missed completely. '*Are* you going to investigate me?'

'Well, not right now,' Kling said.

Carella cleared his throat.

'Who was Mr Leyden's superior?' he asked.

'You'll want to talk to Joe Witters, I guess,' the girl said. To Kling, she said, 'My name's Anne Gilroy, you can remember it by saying "Gilroy was here" '.

'I thought it was *Kilroy*,' Kling said.

'Yes, it used to be. But that was before *I* arrived on the scene.'

'Oh, I see.'

'*Do* you?' she said.

'Yes, I think so, Miss Gilroy.'

'I'll buzz Mr Witters,' she said. 'What did you say your names were?'

'Detectives Carella and Kling,' Carella said.

'Which of you is Carella?'

'Me,' Carella said.

'Which means you're Kling,' Anne said.

'Yes.'

'How nice,' she said, and lifted the phone.

Carella cleared his throat again.

'Mr Witters,' Anne said into the phone, 'there are two gentlemen here from the police, they'd like to talk to you about Andy Leyden. Shall I send them in?' She listened, her blue eyes wide. 'Yes, Mr Witters. Fine,' she said, and hung up. 'You can go right in. I'll show you where it is.' She swung her legs from behind the desk, smiled, and stood up. The miniskirt ended some three inches above her knees. A wide red belt cinched her waist, a pink blouse billowed above it, long blonde hair trailed down her back to somewhere below her shoulder blades. She had seemed like nineteen while seated behind the desk, but her practised walk as she preceded them down the long corridor, fierce little behind jiggling, caused Carella to revise his estimate to twenty-four or -five. Every now and then, she glanced back over her

28

shoulder to make certain Kling was watching her. He was. At the door to Mr Witters' office, she paused, smiled at Kling, twisted the doorknob, and then stood in the doorway so that both detectives had to squeeze past her.

'Gentlemen,' Witters said, and watched Anne Gilroy as she stepped out of the room, closing the door behind her. 'Nymphomaniac,' he commented abruptly, and then said, 'I understand you're here to ask some questions about Andy Leyden.'

'Yes, sir, we are,' Carella said.

'Well, my name's Joe Witters, as I guess you already know. I haven't got *your* names.'

'Carella.'

'Kling.'

Witters shook hands with both of them. He was a white-haired man in his middle fifties, his complexion florid, his eyes a speckled green. There were liver spots on the backs of his huge hands. Monogrammed gold links showed on each cuff of his shirt, and a monogrammed gold oval held his tie in place. He had a habit of wiping his cupped hand downward past his upper lip and over his chin, as though he were smoothing an invisible moustache and beard. His speech was Midwestern, his manner distant. He seemed terribly pressed for time, even though there was not a single scrap of paper on his desk.

'What do you want to know?' he asked.

'How long did Andrew Leyden work for American Tractor and Machine?'

'Close to ten years.'

'What sort of work?'

'Salesman,' Witters said.

'Was he on the road a lot?'

'That's right.'

'How often?'

'Six months of every year, I'd say.'

'How much was he earning?'

'Thirty-five thousand. Plus expenses. Plus stock benefits.'

'He was high-salaried, then.'

29

'That's right.'

'Was he a good salesman?'

'That's right, one of the best.'

'Know anyone who might have wanted him dead, Mr Witters?'

'Nope.'

'Did *you* like him?'

'Personally?'

'Yes, personally.'

'Not too much.' Witters paused. 'I don't like *anyone* too much, you want to know the truth.'

'What's your position with American Tractor and ...'

'Call it AT & M, not such a mouthful,' Witters said.

'AT & M,' Carella said.

'I'm executive vice-president in charge of sales,' Witters said.

'And were you Leyden's immediate superior?'

'Well, we have a sales manager, but he's on the road right now, up in Canada.'

'Any rivalry between him and Leyden?'

'None that I was aware of.'

'Between Leyden and any of the other salesmen?'

'Always rivalry between salesmen,' Witters said. 'That's what makes for good sales. Don't know any of them who'd want to *kill* each other, though. That'd be carrying rivalry a bit far, wouldn't it?' He smiled abruptly. The smile vanished so quickly that neither Kling nor Carella was sure it had been there at all. Witters immediately passed his hand downward over his mouth and chin, as though anxious to wipe away any remnants of it.

'Leyden wasn't up for another man's job ...'

'No.'

'... or after another man's territory ...'

'No.'

'... or edging anyone out of a promotion he ...'

'No.'

'Nothing like that?' Carella said.

'Nothing like that,' Witters said.

30

'Would you say he got along well with his fellow workers?' Kling asked.

'I would say so, yes.'

'Any tension between him and any of the other men?'

'Not that I know of.'

'Was he fooling around with any of the girls in the office?'

'How do you mean?'

'You know.' Kling shrugged. 'Fooling around.'

'No more than usual. They're all nymphomaniacs anyway,' Witters said.

'By "no more than usual", Mr Witters, exactly what? ...'

'Oh, you know. A feel here and there. I don't think he was having an affair with anybody, if that's what you mean.'

'Nothing like that?' Kling said.

'Nothing like that,' Witters said.

'By "nymphomaniacs", Mr Witters, exactly what? ...'

'*All* of them,' Witters said.

'Nymphomaniacs?' Carella said.

'Yes.'

'You mean ...'

'Oh, these short skirts and tight blouses. All nymphomaniacs.'

'I see,' Carella said.

'I wonder if we could see Mr Leyden's office,' Kling said. 'Go through his desk, look at his papers. There may be something there we can ...'

'Well, I don't know as you'll find anything. He's been on the road, you know, and it's our policy to forward all of a salesman's mail to wherever he may be.'

'What was his territory, Mr Witters?'

'California, Oregon, Washington, State of.'

'When did he get back from his last trip?' Carella asked.

'Not supposed to *be* back,' Witters said.

'I beg your pardon, what? ...'

'I said he wasn't supposed to *be* back. Last we got from him was a wire from San Francisco saying he was moving on up to Portland on Monday. That's today. So next thing

31

is he gets killed in his own apartment on Saturday night, when he's still supposed to be in Frisco.'

'When did he send this wire?'

'We got it before close of business last Friday.'

'And he said he was remaining in San Francisco for the weekend?'

'I can get you the wire, if you'd like to see it.'

'Yes, we'd like to see it,' Kling said.

Witters sighed and pressed a button on his intercom. 'Gerry,' he said, 'will you dig out the wire Andy Leyden sent us last week? Bring it right in when you've got it.' He clicked off, abruptly muttered 'nymphomaniac', and then wiped his hand over his mouth and chin again.

'Why do you suppose he came back so suddenly?' Carella asked.

'Beats me. He'd only been gone a month, still had Oregon and Washington to cover, don't ask *me* why he hurried on back.' A knock sounded on the door. 'Come in, come in,' Witters called, and the door opened. A mousy-looking woman of about forty, bespectacled, wearing a grey tweed suit, came into the room, walked awkwardly and self-consciously to the desk, handed the wire to Witters, smiled in embarrassment at both detectives, and hastily walked out again. The door whispered shut behind her.

'Nymphomaniac,' Witters said, and glanced cursorily at the wire. 'Here,' he said. 'This is it.'

Carella took the extended telegram.

'Is this usual?' Carella asked.

'Is *what* usual?'

'Do your salesmen usually keep you informed of their whereabouts?'

'Yes, of course.'

'By telegram?'

'Most of the men phone us every Friday afternoon. Andy generally sent telegrams.'

'Why?'

'I don't know. Guess he didn't like talking on the telephone.'

'Is this also usual? Asking the office to phone his wife and ...'

'Oh, sure, they all do that.'

'Have you any idea why he might have needed his cheque-book?'

'Probably ran out of cheques,' Witters said, and shrugged.

'I thought he had an expense account.'

'He did. Lots of places won't take credit cards, though. In which case our men on the road are instructed to keep a record of what they spend. The firm, of course, makes good later. Cheques are a handy way of keeping a record.'

'Mmm,' Carella said. He handed the telegram back to Witters. 'And this was the last you heard from him, is that right?'

'That's right,' Witters said.

'So you thought he was still in San Francisco.'

'Says right in the wire he'll be holding there for the week-end.'

'And his *wife* thought he was in San Francisco, too, is that right?'

'Well, sure, I guess so. Asked us to call her, so I guess we took care of it, and I guess she assumed he was still out there. As I told you, he'd only been gone a month or so. Swing through California takes at least a month all by itself.'

'Do you suppose he called to let her know he was heading back?'

'Knowing Andy, he probably sent her a telegram,' Witters said, and smiled again, and again wiped the smile away with his hand.

'Mmm,' Carella said. 'Well, could we look at his office now?'

'Sure, but you're not likely to find much on his desk.'

'Perhaps *in* it.'

'Nor *in* it, neither. Andy Leyden's office was pretty much in his hat. He was a travelling man.'

As Witters had promised, there was nothing they could use in Andrew Leyden's desk. His office was at the far end of the corridor, a tiny cubicle painted beige and set between the Mailing Room and the Records Office. A large window faced the street, an air conditioner in its lower half. A brown-chalk drawing of a woman's head, a Picasso print, was framed and hanging on the wall opposite the desk. A cartoon clipped from a magazine was pinned to a bulletin board near the light switch. It showed a woman talking to a salesman on her doorstep, and the caption was, 'Don't you dare try to sell brushes to me, Harry. I'm your *wife!*' The word 'brushes' had a line drawn through it, and over it someone had lettered in the word 'tractors'. In the same handwriting, lettered in over the name 'Harry', someone had written 'Andrew'.

Leyden's desk was made of metal, painted green, completely utilitarian and hardly aesthetic. A picture of his wife was on the left-hand corner of the desk, alongside the telephone. It had been taken prior to a wedding or a ball, and Rose Leyden was wearing a low-cut evening gown. A beauty spot clearly showed just above her left breast, an inch or so higher than the top of her gown. She was smiling stiffly at the photographer. A blotter was the only other

34

thing on the desk. Carella automatically checked it for any mirror writing that might have been left on it, but the blotter seemed new, with only a single inkstain in one corner. The top drawer of the desk contained paper clips and a memo pad and several pencils and an eraser. An AT & M order form was at the back of the drawer. The three side drawers of the desk contained, in sequence: telephone directories for Isola, Calm's Point, and Riverhead; four lined yellow composition pads; a pair of scuffed loafers; a paperback copy of *Hawaii*; a calendar, the top leaf of which still read September 3rd; and a half-full box of chocolates. That was it. They thanked Mr Witters for his time and his courtesy and went down the corridor again towards the elevators. Anne Gilroy looked up as they approached her desk.

'In case I think of anything,' she said to Kling, 'how can I reach you?'

'Are you liable to think of anything?' Carella asked.

'Who knows?' Anne said, and smiled at Kling.

'Here's my card,' Kling said, and fished it from his wallet.

'Bertram,' she said, reading the card. 'I don't know a single person in the entire world named Bertram.'

'Well *now* you do,' Carella said.

'Yes,' she said, looking at Kling. 'Now I do.'

When they got back to the squad room, Andy Parker told them the FBI had sent a teletyped report of the fingerprints dispatched to them last Saturday. They had nothing on Rose or Andrew Leyden, and they had also come up negative on the wild prints. This meant that the killer, whoever he was, had no police record, nor had he ever served in the armed forces of the United States. It also meant, for whatever such information was worth at the moment, that the killer had probably never held a government job either, since most government agencies required fingerprints of their employees. By twelve noon that Monday, it looked as though the case was not going to be such a push over.

The shotgun found in the dead man's hands had been a

12-gauge pump type fitted with a barrel for 2¾-inch shells. Its capacity was six shells. Two of those had been blasted into the face of Rose Leyden, and another two into the face of her husband. A spent cartridge case, unejected, had been found in the receiver of the gun. Two unfired shells were below, waiting to be pumped into the chamber. The shells were 12-gauge Remington Express with Number 2 shot, the largest shot available. Two such loads fired into anyone's face at close range were entirely capable of causing complete destruction. The Police Laboratory had identified the weapon for Carella and also provided him with a manufacturer's serial number. At ten minutes after twelve that Monday, he called the manufacturer's representative in the city, gave him the serial number of the gun, and asked if he could tell him which retail outlet had sold it. The man on the phone asked him to wait a moment, and then came back to the phone and said he would have to look it up, and could he call Carella back? Carella gave him the number at the squad room, and then sent out for a Western on a hard roll. He had finished the sandwich and was drinking his second cup of coffee when the telephone rang.

'Eighty-seventh Squad, Carella,' he said.

'Mr Carella, this is Fred Thiessen.'

'Hello, Mr Thiessen,' Carella said. 'Did you come up with anything?'

'Yes, I have. Let me just check that serial number again, may I? I don't want to make any mistakes on this.'

'It was A-37426,' Carella said.

'A-37426,' Thiessen said. 'Yes, that's what I've got. Well, I checked our invoices for the month of August, which was when that series must have gone out to retailers. We're already shipping the 376s, in this area at least, so I figured this must have been August or so.'

'Was it?'

'Yes. We shipped that gun – it's our 833K, by the way – together with a .410-gauge single-shot, and two bolt-action repeaters. This was on August 4th.'

'To whom did you ship it?'

'Oh, yes, we also shipped our new 20-gauge model, with the selective choke tube, on that same date.'

'To whom, Mr Thiessen?'

'The shipment went to Paramount Sporting Goods.'

'In Isola?'

'No, sir. In Newfield. Across the river, in the next state.'

'Would you have the address handy?'

'Yes, it's 1147 Barter.'

'Well, thank you very much, Mr Thiessen, you've been very helpful.'

'Was one of the guns used in a crime?'

'I'm afraid so,' Carella said.

'We'd appreciate it if our company name wasn't mentioned to the Press.'

'We don't generally release that kind of information anyway, Mr Thiessen.'

'Thank you.'

'Thank *you*,' Carella said again, and hung up.

The fact that the shotgun had been purchased in the town of Newfield, across the river, seemed to indicate that the murderer knew at least *something* about gun laws. For whereas these laws varied widely throughout the US of A, making it possible for hunters (or sometimes murderers) to buy weapons either here or there with relative ease, the law in the city for which Carella and Kling worked was quite stringent. It required that anyone wishing to possess or purchase a rifle or a shotgun needed a permit, and it specifically denied such permit to:

(1) Anyone under the age of eighteen, or
(2) Anyone who had been convicted of a felony or a misdemeanour, or
(3) Anyone who had been confined to a hospital for mental illness, alcoholism, or drug addiction unless now declared sound by a specialist in psychiatric medicine, or
(4) Anyone who suffered from any physical defect which

would make it unsafe for him to handle such weapons, or

(5) Anyone who was a mental defective or a habitual drunkard or a narcotics addict, or

(6) Anyone who had been dishonourably discharged from the military service by reason of an action found constituting a felony or a misdemeanour.

Moreover, application for a permit had to be accompanied by two photographs taken within thirty days prior to filing, and fingerprinting of the applicant was mandatory.

It was a tough law, and a good law.

In the town of Newfield, however, across the river, you could buy a rifle or a shotgun over the counter of any store selling them, so long as you had the money necessary to complete this act of commerce. If you chose to carry the weapon back across the river and into the city, the law required that application for a permit be made within forty-eight hours and that the gun be left at your resident precinct until you could produce the proper permit and registration certificate. But if you had bought a shotgun in Newfield and intended to shoot two people in the face, it is doubtful that you would even consider registering the gun once you got back to the city.

Paramount Sporting Goods was in a downtown section of Newfield, in a triangular-shaped business area bordered by Chinatown, the railroad marshalling yards, and an Italian ghetto. The owner of the shop was a pleasant moon-faced man named Abe Feldman. When they walked in, he was assembling an order for a high-school football team, assorting jerseys according to size, stacking shoulder pads and mouthpieces, his counter covered with all the plastic armour needed in that warlike game. Carella and Kling introduced themselves, and Feldman immediately looked worried.

'What's the matter?' he asked. 'What's happened?'

'This has nothing to do with *you*, Mr Feldman. We're investigating a murder and ...'

'Oh, my God!' Feldman said.

'... we have reason to believe the murder weapon was purchased in your store. I wonder ...'

'Oh, my God!' he said again.

'... I wonder if you'd be able to dig out your sales slips ...'

'When was it?' Feldman asked.

'Well, the gun was shipped to you on August 4th, so it would have to be any time after that.'

'August?'

'Yes.'

'I already got my slips for August and September put away.'

'Would they be difficult to get at?'

'Well, I got them in the back. There's such a *chazerai* back there, believe me, I hate to go in there sometimes.'

'Well, this ...'

'Also, you caught me right in the middle. I got a whole football team here I'm trying to get ready.'

'Well, this is a murder case,' Kling said gently.

'*This* is murder right here,' Feldman said, indicating the equipment covering the counter top. 'All right, come on. If *you* can stand it, *I* can stand it.'

The back of Feldman's shop was a monument to disorder. Cartons were heaped haphazardly upon other cartons, hockey sticks were stacked in corners, ice skates and boxing gloves hung from nails and pegs, skis and poles leaned dangerously against the walls, fishing poles wobbled overhead on wooden slats, boxes of pingpong balls and jackknives teetered menacingly, dust covered everything.

'Oh boy, what a mess,' Feldman said. 'Every time I come back here, I get an ulcer. August, you said?'

'Or any time since.'

'Oh boy,' Feldman said. 'August, August, where the hell is August?'

He blew dust off a box of fishing flies, put it back on a shelf that contained athletic supporters, reached for an-

39

other box, blew dust from it, shook his head, said, 'No, that's July', and picked up yet another box. 'What the hell is *this*?' he asked of no one, nodded, said, 'BB pellets', put the box back on the shelf alongside a box of hockey pucks, lifted another large box, and said, 'September. You want to start with September?'

'Why not?' Carella said.

'Where the hell am I going to put this?' Feldman said, looking around. He found a large carton containing baseball bats, rested the box on it, and lifted the lid. The box was crammed full of sales slips, thirty or forty of which fell to the dusty floor when he raised the lid.

'There must be ten thousand in this box alone,' Feldman said.

'Well, not *that* many,' Carella said, and smiled.

'All right, *five* thousand, who's counting?'

'Do you record serial numbers when you sell a gun?' Kling asked.

'Every time,' Feldman said. 'That's the law in this state.'

'For pistols, it is,' Carella said. 'How about shotguns?'

'No, I don't record no serial numbers on shotguns.' Feldman looked worried again. 'I'm not required to do that, am I?'

'No, but ... '

'No, I don't do that,' Feldman said. 'Why? You got a serial number?'

'Yes.'

'It won't do you no good here,' Feldman said, and shook his head.

'How about the model number? Would you write that on your invoice?'

'Sure I write the model number. Besides, I won't sell any kind of gun to somebody I don't know. Unless he gives me his name and address.'

Carella nodded. Kling gave Feldman the manufacturer's name and the model number of the shotgun – 833K – and the three men began wading through the sales slips. There were exactly five hundred and twenty-seven slips in the box; Kling counted them. Not one of them recorded a sale for a model 833K shotgun.

'So it must have been August,' Carella said.

'Just our luck,' Feldman said. He was a determined little man, and he seemed to have entered into the spirit of the chase now, anxious to find the sales slip, anxious to be of assistance in bringing a murderer to justice. Busily, he searched the crowded, dusty back room for the missing box of August sales slips. At last, he found it buried under six boxes of tennis balls on the bottom shelf against the far wall.

Kling began counting again as they went through the August slips. They had reached two hundred and twelve when Feldman said, 'Here we go'.

They looked at the slip.

'See?' Feldman said. 'There's his name and address. I take everybody's name and address when I don't know who it is I'm selling a gun to. You never know when some nut is going to shoot the President, am I right?'

The name on the sales slip was Walter Damascus. The address listed was 234 South Second Street. The price of the gun was $74.95, plus the five per cent sales tax, and the two per cent city sales tax.

'Would you have sold more than one of these models?' Kling said.

'In August, you mean?'

'Yes.'

'No, how *could* I? I only got one in the shipment.'

'Then this is the man who bought it,' Carella said.

'Sure, it must be.'

'Sounds like a phoney name,' Kling said. 'Damascus.'

'Did you ask him for identification, Mr Feldman?' Carella asked.

'Well, no, I didn't.'

'Why not?'

'I never do.'

'When you sell a stranger a gun, you take his name and address ...'

'Yes.'

'... but you don't ask for identification?'

'No.'

'Well, what good is *that*?' Carella asked.

'I never thought of it,' Feldman said, and shrugged. 'I'm not required to ask them for *anything*, you know. You can buy a rifle or a shotgun anywhere you want to in this state without a licence, without *nothing*. I just ask them their name and address as a precaution, you understand me? Just in case some *nut* is buying the gun, you know what I mean?'

'Yes, we know what you mean,' Carella said.

FOUR

TWO HUNDRED AND THIRTY-FOUR South Second Street was a corner building, a red-brick tenement that at one time must have been very posh. Gargoyles still leered into the street from each floor, and even the entrance doorway was decorated with a sculpted keystone, a woman's head with the nose gone and the word S U C K painted in blue across her mouth. Two men were standing on the front stoop when Carella and Kling entered the building. Instantly smelling fuzz, they watched as the two cops studied the mailboxes in the foyer. Neither of them said a word.

The mailboxes listed a W. Damascus for apartment 31.

There were slum smells on the stairwell, slum sounds in the halls and behind closed doors and in the airshaft between the building and the one adjacent. There was a sense of life contained and concealed, a teeming, tumultuous life breeding in the cracks of poverty, eating and mating and sleeping and excreting, an animalistic substructure dwelling in a multi-layered cave that stank of piss and frying fat. On the second floor, a rat the size of an alley cat stared at Carella and Kling with eyes that glittered in the refracted airshaft light pouring through the stairwell window. Carella, who had already drawn his revolver, almost fired in reflex. Boldly, the rat held his ground and continued to stare at them. They sidled past him, close to the banister, and the rat's head turned, nose twitching, alert, watching. Carella was sweating when they reached the third floor.

Apartment 31 was in the middle of the hallway, next to 32, and facing 33. Kling listened at the door, shook his head, and then backed off against the opposite wall. Carella moved to the side of the door, revolver in hand, finger inside the trigger guard. Kling raised his knee, shoved himself

43

off the opposite wall, and piston-kicked the flat of his foot against the door, as high as he could, as close to the lock and the jamb as he could. The lock sprang, the door swung inward on its hinges. Kling followed the door into the room, and Carella peeled off like the wingman in a fighter squadron, crouching low, gun in hand, immediately behind Kling.

The room was empty.

They fanned out immediately, going through all of the rooms in succession. The bathroom door was closed. Carella slowly turned the knob with his left hand, flipped the door suddenly open, and entered the tiny room gun-first. It, too, was empty.

'You'd better get the super up here,' he said to Kling. 'I'll take a look around.'

The apartment was small and determinedly filthy. The door Kling had kicked in opened on a living-room furnished with a three-piece 'suite' (one armchair upholstered in gold, another in blue, the sofa in maroon) clustered around a television set in the corner. A picture of a smiling peasant puffing on a pipe, neo-Rembrandt, was hanging over the television set. An open edition of the city's only morning tabloid lay on the sofa. The date on the paper was September 9th. There were empty beer cans and full ashtrays on the floor. In the kitchen, dishes caked with the leftovers of a week's meals were stacked in the sink, and used breakfast dishes were still on the table. Judging from the dry and mouldy cornflakes still clinging to the bottom of the bowl, the last breakfast Damascus had eaten here could easily have been close to two months ago, the date on the living-room newspaper. A September issue of *Life* was on the bathroom floor, near the toilet bowl. A man's safety razor was on the sink, and patches of dried, hair-clogged shaving cream clung to the sloping tile sides. Wherever Damascus had gone, he had not bothered to take his razor with him. Two small scraps of toilet tissue were near the cold-water faucet, each with small smears of blood on them. It was reasonable to assume that Damascus had cut himself while shaving, and had used the toilet tissue to

44

blot the blood. A grimy ring circled the bathtub. A sliver of Ivory soap and a swirl of hair were caught in the open drain. Near one claw leg of the old-fashioned tub, a man's striped undershorts were waddled in a ball. There were cockroaches nesting behind a tube of toothpaste on the sink, and tile lice wiggled on the floor. It was altogether the most charming room in the place.

The bedroom ran a close second.

The bed had been slept in and left unmade. There were grease stains on the pillow, and the sheets were splotched here and there with what might have been semen stains. Alongside the bed, on the nightstand, there was an open box of Trojans. According to the printing on the box, there should have been three contraceptives in it. Carella shook them out on to the bed. There were only two condoms in the box. The bed stank of sweat and God knew what. The entire room stank. Carella went to the window and opened it wide. On the fire escape outside, there was an empty milk bottle and an empty graham-cracker carton. In the apartment across the airshaft, a young housewife in a flowered dress was busily cleaning her kitchen and singing *Penny Lane*. Carella took a deep breath and turned away from the window.

The only closet in the room contained a pile of dirty shirts and underwear on the floor, and a brown suit hanging on the clothes bar. Carella checked the label and was surprised to discover the suit had come from one of the more exclusive men's shops in town. A grey fedora rested on the shelf over the clothes bar. In the far corner of the shelf, Carella found an open box containing an Iver Johnson .22-calibre revolver and seventeen Peters .22-calibre cartridges.

A bottle with perhaps three fingers of Scotch left in it was on the bedroom dresser. Two glasses were beside it. One had lipstick stains on the rim. A matchbox carrying advertising for the A & P was on the dresser top, together with a crumpled Winston cigarette package. Carella was opening the top dresser drawer when Kling came in with the superintendent of the building.

45

The super was a Negro, perhaps forty-five years old, with a clubfoot and suspicious brown eyes. He wore work denims and a black cardigan sweater. The expression on his face clearly stated that he resented having been born black with the additional handicap of a clubfoot. He did not like white people, and he did not like healthy people, and he did not like cops, and here he was in a stinking tenement flat about to be questioned by two men who were white healthy cops.

'This is the super,' Kling said. 'His name's Henry Yancy.'

'How do you do, Mr Yancy?' Carella said. 'I'm Detective Carella, and this is my partner, Detective Kling.'

'I already met your partner,' Yancy said.

'We'd like to ask you a few questions, if we may.'

'Do I have a choice?' Yancy said.

'We simply want to know a few things about the occupant of this apartment.'

'What do you want to know?' Yancy said. 'Make it fast because I got to get down and take in the garbage cans before I get a ticket from the cop on the beat.'

'We'll try to be brief,' Carella said. 'Who rents this apartment?'

'Walter Damascus.'

'How long has he lived here?'

'Must be three, four years.'

'Is he married?'

'No.'

'Does he live here alone?'

'Well,' Yancy said, and shrugged. 'He lives here alone, but he has women coming in whenever he's here.'

'Isn't he here all the time?'

'Not too much.'

'How often is he here?'

'He's in and out, on and off. I don't ask nobody nothing long as they pay their rent.'

'*Does* he pay his rent?'

'The owner of the building never said nothing about him, so I guess he pays his rent. I'm just the super here.'

'When's the last time you saw him?'

'I don't recall.'

'Was it recently?'

'I don't recall.'

'Would it have been in September sometime?'

'I told you I don't recall.'

'Mr Yancy, we'd hate to have to bother all the people on this floor, just to find out when Damascus was here last.'

'That's your job, ain't it?' Yancy said, and paused. 'Bothering people?'

'Our job right now,' Kling said flatly, 'is trying to locate the suspect in a murder case. *That's* our job.'

'Who got killed?' Yancy asked.

'Why should that matter to you?' Carella said.

'It don't,' Yancy answered, and shrugged.

'Try to remember when you saw Damascus last, will you?'

'After the summer sometime.'

'Before Labour Day?'

'Yeah, I guess so.'

'At the beginning of September, then?'

'I guess so.'

'Have you seen him since?'

'I ain't even sure I seen him then.'

'Did you see him at all this month?'

'No.'

'Not at any time during the month of October, is that right?'

'That's right.'

'But you *did* see him in September, and you think it was some time before Labour Day.'

'Yeah, I guess so.'

'Was he alone?'

'There was a woman with him.'

'Do you know who she was?'

'No. He always has a different woman with him.'

'Had you ever seen this one before?'

'Once or twice.'

'But you don't know her name.'

'No.'

'What'd she look like?'

'I don't recall.'

'Was she white or black?'

'White,' Yancy said.

'What colour hair?'

'Red.'

'Eyes?'

'I don't recall.'

'Was she pretty?'

'For a white woman,' Yancy said.

'How old would you say she was?'

'Thirty, something like that.'

'Is she from the neighbourhood?'

'I don't think so. Only time I ever seen her was when Damascus brought her around.'

'Which was often, you said.'

'Well, a few times, anyway.'

'How old is Damascus?'

'In his forties,' Yancy said.

'What does he look like?'

'Oh, he's about your height, six feet or so, dark hair and blue eyes, nice-looking fellow.'

'You getting this, Bert?' Carella asked.

'Mm-huh,' Kling said, without looking up from his pad.

'Is he white?' Carella asked.

'He's white,' Yancy said.

'What kind of complexion?'

'I told you. White.'

'Pale, dark, fair, sallow?'

'Fair, I guess.'

'How is he built?'

'About like your partner here.'

'Does he have a moustache or a beard?'

'No.'

'Any scars?'

'No scars.'

'Tattoos?'

48

'No tattoos.'

'Any sort of distinctive mark?'

'No sort of marks,' Yancy said.

'Is he deformed in any way?'

'You mean does he have a clubfoot?' Yancy asked.

'That's not what I meant, sir,' Carella said, refusing to flinch.

'No, he isn't deformed,' Yancy said.

'What about his voice? What kind of voice does he have?'

'I don't know.'

'Gruff, soft, refined, effeminate?'

'He's not a fairy.'

'Does he lisp or stutter?'

'No, he talks straight out. Soft, I guess you would say. And fast. He talks very fast.'

'Bert?' Carella said. 'Anything else?'

'Jewellery.'

'Does he habitually wear any rings or other jewellery?' Carella asked.

'He's got a ring with his initial on it,' Yancy said.

'Which initial? W or D?'

'W.'

'Does he wear it on his right hand or his left?'

'His right, I think.'

'Any other jewellery?'

'An ID bracelet, I think.'

'Gold or silver?'

'Silver.'

'With his name on it?'

'I never saw it close up,' Yancy said.

'Would you know whether or not Damascus is employed?'

'I don't know. I'm just the super here.'

'You're doing very well, Mr Yancy,' Carella said.

'You've given us an excellent description so far,' Kling said

Yancy looked at them suspiciously. He was used to all sorts of bullshit from Whitey, and he nodded sceptically now, letting the detectives know he wasn't about to be that easily flattered.

'I *still* got to get my garbage cans off the sidewalk,' he said flatly.

'We'll straighten out any problems with the cop on the beat,' Carella promised.

'Sure. You'll pay the fine, too, I suppose.'

'There won't be any fine, Mr Yancy. Try to remember whether or not Damascus leaves the house and returns at any regularly set times, would you?'

'When he's here, do you mean?'

'Yes.'

'If he's got a job, it must be nights,' Yancy said. 'Only time I ever seen him around was during the day.'

'He leaves the apartment at night?'

'I guess so.'

'What time?'

'Eight, nine o'clock, something like that.'

'But you wouldn't know where he goes?'

'No.'

'Thank you, Mr Yancy.'

'That it?'

'That's it, thank you.'

They watched as he limped towards the doorway. At the door, he turned and said, 'Aint nothing wrong with my eyes'.

'What?' Carella said.

'The description,' Yancy answered, and went out.

Carella went to the dresser. In the top drawer, in a box containing tie clasps and cuff links, he found an uncancelled cheque made out to Walter Damascus for one hundred and ten dollars and seventy-nine cents. The cheque was drawn to the account of The Cozy Corners and signed by someone named Daniel Cudahy.

'Something?' Kling asked.

'I think so,' Carella answered.

The Cozy Corners was a bar-cum-nightclub on Dover Plains Avenue in Riverhead. The owner's name was

Daniel Cudahy, and when Carella and Kling got there at five in the afternoon, he was eating his dinner.

'In this crazy racket,' he said, 'you got to eat when you get a chance. It starts becoming a madhouse around here in a little while.'

Cudahy was a diminutive man with a balding head and a broken nose. There was a knife scar on his right temple, and his right eye twitched spasmodically as though in memory of how close the knife had come to gouging it. He sat at a table near the bar, eating a minute steak and French fries, sipping a bottle of Heineken's beer. The decor of the place was cosy-cute, with chequerboard tablecloths and wood panelling and phoney electric candlesticks on each table. A small dance floor was at one end of the room, a piano, a set of drums, and three music stands behind it. The name of the band performing – according to what was lettered on the bass drum – was KEN MURPHY'S MARAUDERS The detectives sat at Cudahy's invitation and watched him demolish the steak. Between mouthfuls, he said, 'Sure, I know Wally. Where the hell *is* that bum?'

'He works for you, does he?'

'He's my bouncer,' Cudahy said.

'Does he work full time?'

'Every night except Sunday. We're closed Sunday.'

'When'd you see him last, Mr Cudahy?'

'Friday night. He was supposed to come in Saturday night, and never showed. I'm expecting him tonight, but who the hell knows?'

'Did he call in?'

'Nope.'

'Did *you* call him?'

'He hasn't got a phone.'

'No place you can reach him?'

'He lives in Isola someplace, some crummy neighbourhood. I wouldn't go down there personally if you gave me a million dollars.'

'He lives on South Second, isn't that right?'

'Yeah, somewhere down there. All full of spics and niggers,' Cudahy said. 'I wouldn't go down there with the National Guard.'

'And he has no phone?'

'No phone.'

'How come?'

'What do you mean, how come?'

'Almost everybody has a phone.'

'Well, he's hardly ever there, what the hell does he need a phone for?'

'If he's not there, where *is* he?' Kling asked.

'Who knows? He *works* for me, that's all. His private life is his own business. I pay him seventy-five bucks a week, and he throws out anybody causing a disturbance. That's our agreement. He can live wherever the hell he wants, in the *park* if he wants, on a park bench, it don't matter to me.'

'Is he married, would you know?'

'If he is, he's sure got it going for him six ways.'

'What do you mean?'

'Well, he's always got broads hanging on him. He's a real handsome guy, you know. I think he wanted to be an actor one time.'

'Has he ever *mentioned* a wife to you?'

'Naw, I think he's single, actually. A guy who looks like he does, why would he want to get married?'

'He was here Friday night, you said?'

'Yeah.'

'From when to when?'

'Got here at nine, left at closing time.'

'Which was when?'

'Two o'clock. We're open till one every weekday night except Friday. Friday it's two, Saturday it's three, and Sunday we're closed. That's it.'

'So he left here at two.'

'That's right. I paid him and he took off.'

'Is this the cheque you gave him?' Carella asked, and took the cheque from his wallet.

'That's it. I pay every two weeks. That's for two weeks' salary less social security, disability, and federal and state

52

withholding. It comes to one hundred and ten dollars and seventy-nine cents.'

'Which means he's been to that apartment some time between Friday night and today,' Kling said.

'Huh?' Cudahy asked again.

'We're just thinking out loud,' Carella said.

'Oh,' Cudahy said, and poured more beer from the bottle into his glass. 'You guys want a drink or something?'

'No, thanks,' Kling said.

'Too early for you?'

'We're not allowed,' Carella said.

'Yeah, sure. I wish I had a nickel for every cop who ain't allowed to drink on duty who comes in here and knocks off three shots in a row. Especially in the wintertime.'

'Well,' Carella said, and shrugged.

'What do you want Wally for? Did he do something?'

'Maybe.'

'Will you let us know if he comes in?' Kling said.

'Sure. What'd he do?'

'He might have killed a few people.'

Cudahy whistled softly and then swallowed some beer.

'Ever see him with a gun?' Kling asked.

'Nope.'

'Didn't wear one on the job, huh?'

'Nope.'

'We're thinking of an Iver Johnson .22,' Carella said.

'I wouldn't know an Iver Johnson .22 from a 1937 Packard,' Cudahy said, and grinned. 'Is that what he killed somebody with?'

'No,' Carella said, and frowned.

'When's he supposed to have done it?' Cudahy asked.

'Friday night sometime.'

'After he left here?'

'Looks like it.'

'You got the wrong man,' Cudahy said flatly.

'What makes you think so?'

'Unless *she* was in it with him.'

'Who?'

53

'The broad.'

'*What* broad?'

'He left here Friday night with some broad.'

'Who?'

'I don't know her name. I seen her around here before, though. She comes to pick him up every now and then. She drives a big yellow Buick.'

'What does she look like?'

'A good-looking tomato,' Cudahy said. 'Red hair, green eyes, everything in the right places.'

'You say she left here with him Friday night?'

'Yeah.'

'At two in the morning?'

'Yep.'

'Did she have the Buick with her?'

'Yeah, she's always got that submarine with her. I think she goes to bed with that goddamn submarine.'

'Did Damascus say where they were going?'

'Where would *you* go with a gorgeous redhead at two o'clock in the morning?' Cudahy asked.

The drive downtown to South Second took exactly forty-two minutes. They made the drive carefully, observing all the speed limits, and then subtracted ten minutes from the total in allowance for what would have been lighter traffic at two o'clock in the morning. This meant that it would have taken Damascus and the redheaded girl approximately a half-hour to get from the Cozy Corners in Riverhead to the apartment on South Second Street. They would have arrived there if that's where they'd been headed, at about two-thirty. The possibility existed, of course, that they had gone instead to the girl's apartment. Or perhaps they had gone directly to the Leyden apartment, where Damascus had pumped four shots into Rose and Andrew – while the girl watched? It sounded incredible, but Carella and Kling were both experienced cops who knew that *nothing* was incredible where murder was concerned.

Henry Yancy was nowhere in sight. They climbed the

steps to the third floor and knocked on the door to apartment 33.

'Who is it?' a woman's voice called.

'Police,' Carella said.

'Oh, shit,' the woman answered.

They waited. They heard footsteps approaching the door, heard a chain being removed from its slotted track, heard the lock being turned. The door opened. The woman was perhaps forty years old, her hair up in curlers and covered with a kerchief. She was wearing a blue apron, and holding a wooden spoon in her hand.

'What is it?' she asked. 'I'm making supper.'

Carella flashed the tin and said, 'We'd like to ask you a few questions'.

'What about? Nobody in this house done nothing.'

'Were you in your apartment on Friday night?'

'We were in all night Friday, my husband and me both. If it's something happened someplace Friday night, we had nothing to do with it.'

'Were you awake at two-thirty?'

'No.'

'Did you hear anyone coming in across the hall at that time?'

'I told you we were asleep.'

'You didn't hear anything in the hall?' Kling asked.

'Do *you* hear things when you're sleeping?' the woman asked.

'Thank you,' Kling said, and the woman slammed the door.

'I keep wondering why he went out to buy a shotgun when he had a perfectly good .22 in his closet,' Carella said.

'I keep wondering a lot of things,' Kling said. 'Let's hit this other apartment, huh?'

The woman in apartment 32 told them she had gone to an American Legion affair on Friday night. She and her husband had not come home until three-thirty in the morning. She said she'd heard nothing unusual in the apartment next door.

55

'Did you hear anything at *all*?' Carella asked.

'No,' she said. 'Nothing.'

'Can you *usually* hear what goes on in there?

'Well,' she said, 'the walls are very thin, you know.'

'Do you think anyone was in there?'

'No. Why, what is it? Was there a burglary? There's been a lot of burglaries in this building lately.'

'No, not a burglary,' Kling said. 'We're trying to find out whether Walter Damascus was in his apartment when you got home Friday night.'

'Well, how *could* he be?' the woman said.

'What do you mean?'

'He was downstairs.'

'Doing what?' Carella asked immediately.

'Getting into a yellow automobile,' the woman said.

So they drove uptown again – this was a day for driving, all right – and they discovered that it took them twenty minutes to get from South Second to the Leyden apartment on South Engels Street, which (again deducting ten minutes for lighter early-morning traffic) meant that Damascus could have left his own apartment at three-thirty, after approximately an hour of dalliance with the unidentified redhead, to arrive at the Leyden apartment by three-forty. Add five minutes for taking the elevator or climbing the steps to the tenth floor, and you had an estimated time of 3.45 AM for the murders. Four shotgun blasts in the dead of night, and nobody reporting them to the police.

Some questions obviously had to be asked.

It was close to seven-thirty; both men were exhausted. They agreed between them that the questions could wait until morning, and Carella called the squad room to say they were signing off. Detective Meyer Meyer, who was catching, said, 'Short day today?' – which was what he usually said no matter what time anyone called in to check out.

His day was just beginning.

The woman had been stabbed.

It wasn't such an exciting stabbing, no exotic sexy stuff or anything like that, just a breadknife stuck in her chest, that's all. She was wearing all her clothes, it was really a pretty routine stabbing. The breadknife had entered at an uplifted angle just below her left breast, the assailant apparently wielding the weapon underhanded rather than attacking with a downward slash. There was a lot of blood all over the kitchen floor (she was lying on her back in front of the sink) and a few broken dishes (apparently her attacker had surprised her in the middle of cleaning up), but it was a pretty run-of-the-mill stabbing, the kind you might expect to get on a Monday night, nothing bizarre or outstanding about it, just a knife sticking out of a dead woman lying on the floor in blood and broken crockery.

Meyer Meyer got to the apartment at three minutes past midnight.

The cop on the beat, a patrolman named Stuart Collister, had phoned in the squeal at 11.55 PM after being accosted by a man on the street who said to him, 'Officer, excuse me for breaking your ear, but there's a dead bird upstairs'. The dead bird was the lady with the knife in her chest. Such a bird, she wasn't. She was all of fifty years old, with large brown eyes that stared up at the ceiling and a generous mouth artfully reduced by the line of her carefully applied lipstick. She was wearing a black dress and a string of pearls and black pumps and black net stockings and she stank to high heaven because she had been dead for some little while. Her colour wasn't too pretty either, because the apartment was a very warm one, with the radiators going full blast, and putrefaction had begun, was in fact well along, so everything smelled and looked terrible, a routine stabbing.

Meyer went outside to talk to the Homicide cops, and then he chatted with the photographer a while, and then he got around to Patrolman Collister, who had held for further questioning the man who'd stopped him on the street.

The man looked too hip for his age: Meyer guessed he

57

was in his early sixties. He was wearing a double-vented blue blazer with brass buttons, beige pipestem slacks, a pale-blue turtleneck sweater, and brown buckskin desert boots. His hair was white, and he combed it the way Julius Caesar must have before he started going bald and took to wearing laurel wreaths. His name was Barnabas Coe, and he was more than eager to tell Meyer exactly how he had discovered the body.

'What's her name, to begin with?' Meyer asked.

'Margie Ryder. Marguerite.'

'How old is she?'

'Fifty-two, I think.'

'Is this her apartment?'

'Yes.'

'All right, let's hear it.'

They stood together just outside the front door of the apartment, the laboratory technicians walking in and out of the place with their equipment now, the medical examiner arriving and saying hello to everyone, the photographer coming out into the hall again to get some more flashbulbs from a leather bag on the corridor floor, the DA's man arriving and saying hello to Meyer and then going over to where the Homicide dicks were telling stories about Stabbings They Had Known. Meyer was a tall man with blue eyes and a bald head, burly in a light-grey top-coat, hatless. The top of Coe's emperor cut was level with Meyer's chin. He kept staring up into Meyer's face as he talked, his head bobbing in emphasis, his blue eyes glowing.

'Margie and I were real tight,' he said. 'Used to have pads across the hall from each other down in The Quarter, this was, oh, 1960, 1961. Never *made* it, you understand, but were tight, man, tight. Crazy bird, that Margie, I really dug her. She finally had to move because the loot was running out; up here, the tab's a lot cheaper.'

'The loot?'

'The insurance loot. Her husband dropped dead just after the war. The *real* war.'

'How'd he die?' Meyer asked suspiciously.

'Lung cancer,' Coe said, and paused. 'Never smoked in his life.'

Meyer nodded. He kept staring at Coe in fascination, studying the hip clothes and hairdo, listening to the jargon, wondering when Coe would reach up to peel off the sixty-year-old rubber mask he was surely wearing, revealing his true teeny-bopper face.

'Anyway,' Coe said, 'we kept the lines open even after she moved. Which is odd, I think, and kind of rare because, whereas The Quarter may not be a garden spot, up here is really the asshole, am I right? I mean, man, cheap is cheap, who wants to live like pigs?'

'Nobody,' Meyer said, and kept staring at the seamed and tired face, the wrinkled flesh around blue eyes that glowed with excitement as Coe told his story.

'Not that *she* lived like a pig,' Coe said. 'That's a nice pad in there.' He gestured with his head towards the open doorway. 'For *here*,' he amended.

'Yes,' Meyer said.

'She used to come downtown every now and then, and I'd pop in here whenever I was in the neighbourhood. She developed a new bag after she moved, writing poetry. Wild, huh?'

'Yeah, wild,' Meyer said.

'She used to read me her stuff whenever I stopped by. *"Oh great mother city, I spit out your naked tits and suck bilge from your sewers instead."* That was one of her lines. Tough, huh?'

'Yeah, tough,' Meyer said. 'How'd you? . . .'

'Well, tonight I had a date with a little Puerto Rican bird who lives on Ainsley, sweet oh sweet, these great big marvellous brown eyes and this lovely tight little bod, oh sweet, man.'

'Yeah,' Meyer said.

'Had to get her home by eleven-thirty, though, very strict parents, I'm surprised they didn't send a *dueña* along. Well, she's only nineteen, I guess you've got to expect that kind of thing with *señoritas*.' Coe winked and smiled. Meyer almost winked back at him.

'So I had time to burn, so I decided to hit Margie's pad, see how she was getting along, maybe listen to some more of her poetry. "*Your hairy incubus startles me*," that was another of her lines. Crazy, huh?'

'Yeah, crazy. So what happened when you got here?'

'I knocked on the door, and there was no answer. So I knocked again, and still no answer. Then, I don't know, I tried the knob. I don't know why I tried it, I just did. Usually, you knock on a door, nobody answers, you figure the party's out, am I right?'

'Right.'

'Instead, I tried the knob, and the door opened. So I called out her name, Margie, I said, and still there was no answer. So I looked in. The place reeked. I couldn't understand that, because Margie always kept everything so neat and clean, you know, almost compulsive. So I went in. And there she was laying on the kitchen floor in basic black and pearls, and there's a blade in her chest.'

'What'd you do?'

'I screamed.'

'Then what?'

'I ran downstairs.'

'And then?'

'I found the local fuzz and told him there was a dead bird up here, Margie. I told him she was dead.' Coe paused. 'You want the *señorita*'s name?' he asked.

'What for?'

'Check out my story,' Coe said, and shrugged. 'Make sure I really *was* with her tonight, instead of up here doing poor Margie.'

'From the looks of poor Margie,' Meyer said, 'I'd be more interested in knowing where you were a *week* ago.'

FIVE

WELL, HIS estimate was a bit off.

He wasn't a medical examiner, he was just a flatfoot, and the look he'd had of Margie Ryder on the kitchen floor seemed to indicate she'd been dead and gone for at least a week.

Not so, the man who did the autopsy reported. The apartment had been very warm, the man said, a condition rare for a slum dwelling in the month of October, most slum landlords preferring to save their thermal output for the dog days of January and February, and being very chary with the heat before the turn of the year. But of course all the windows were closed tight and there had been no traffic in or out of the apartment since the time of the murder, which meant that whatever heat did come up in the radiators had been contained and had therefore speeded up the putrefaction and decomposition of poor Margie Ryder.

Friday night was what the medical examiner reported.

Friday night was when the poor bird had been done in, give or take several hours in consideration of human error in trying to deal with variables like heat in slum apartments. Meyer wondered how the city ever hoped to handle the population explosion when all a slum dweller could do after eleven o'clock on any winter's night was crawl into bed to seek a little body warmth? He then wondered whether or not Margie Ryder had sought a little body warmth last Friday night, and put the question to the medical examiner, who promptly reported that they'd found no trace of semen in the vaginal vault. Besides, the poor bird had been found fully dressed, her clothing neither torn nor disarrayed; somebody had just stuck a knife in her, that's all, a routine stabbing.

Meyer said goodbye to the medical examiner. He had come on duty at 4 PM that Tuesday afternoon, and it was now 4.30, and he figured he'd better get cracking on the case. So he buzzed the lieutenant's office and asked Byrnes who'd be working it with him, and Byrnes said Cotton Hawes. They were about to leave the squad room to head for the Ryder apartment, when a man appeared at the slatted wooden railing that divided the squad room from the corridor outside.

'I want to talk to whoever's handling the Margie Ryder case,' he said.

'*I'm* handling it,' Meyer answered.

'Can I come in?'

'Sure,' Meyer said, and rose to open the gate for him. The man was carrying a topcoat over his arm, and he held a grey fedora in his hand. He looked ill at ease in a blue business suit, as though he had dressed especially for his visit to the police station and would have been more comfortable in a sports jacket or a sweater. He took the chair Meyer offered him, and then watched Hawes as he pulled another chair over to the desk.

'I'm Detective Meyer,' Meyer said. 'This is Detective Hawes. We're working the case together.'

'I'm Jim Martin,' the man said. He was a big man, with broad shoulders and a square, craggy face, brown hair worn in a severe military cut, eyes so dark they seemed black, huge-knuckled hands, the hands of a street brawler. He was sitting beside Hawes, who was six feet two inches tall and weighed two hundred pounds, and yet he seemed to dwarf him, seemed ready to bulge free of his tightly restraining blue confirmation suit, explode muscularly into the squad room or perhaps the entire building. There was a nervous undercurrent to this man, the way he clenched and unclenched his enormous hands, the way he kept wetting his lips, his dark eyes darting from Hawes to Meyer, as though uncertain to whom he would tell his story. The detectives waited patiently. At last, Meyer said, 'Yes, Mr Martin?'

'I knew her,' Martin said.

'You knew Mrs Ryder?'

'I didn't know she was married,' Martin said.

'A widow. Her husband died shortly after the war.'

'I didn't know that.'

He fell silent again. He clenched his right hand and then his left. His fedora dropped to the floor, and he picked it up and then looked apologetically at Hawes, who was watching him intently.

'You knew her,' Meyer prompted.

'Yes.'

'How?'

'I'm a bartender.'

Meyer nodded. 'Where do you work, Mr Martin?'

'Over at Perry's. Do you know it? It's on DeBeck.'

'Yes, we're familiar with it,' Hawes said.

'I read in the paper this morning that somebody stabbed her,' Martin said, and again dropped his hat. Hawes retrieved it for him, and he mumbled a 'Thank you', and then turned to Meyer again. 'I don't want to get anybody in trouble,' he said.

The detectives waited.

'But she was a nice lady, Margie, and I can't see how anyone who knew her could have done a thing like this.'

'Yes?' Meyer said.

'I know you guys don't need any help from me, I'm just a bartender. I never even read a mystery in my entire life.'

'Go on,' Meyer said.

'But . . . well, look, the newspaper this morning said nothing was touched in the apartment, so that lets out a burglar. And whoever stabbed her, he didn't . . . well, somebody on the scene said it didn't look like rape had been the motive. I forget who said it, somebody from the District Attorney's office. So what I mean is this wasn't somebody who *broke* into her apartment, you know what I mean? If it wasn't burglary, and it wasn't rape, then . . .'

'Yes, we're following you, Mr Martin.'

'Well, if it wasn't a *criminal*, if it wasn't somebody who *broke* in to do some criminal thing, then it had to be somebody she knew, right?'

'Go on.'

'Well, anybody who *really* knew Margie would never do a thing like this. She was a sweet, decent person that if you knew her you couldn't think of ever harming her. She was a *lady*,' Martin said.

'So what do you think?'

'I think it had to be somebody who *didn't* know her.'

'But you said . . .'

'I mean didn't know her *good*. A stranger.'

'I see.'

'A stranger,' Martin repeated, and fell silent again. 'Jesus, I hate to get anybody in trouble, I mean it. I may be all wet about this.'

'What's your idea?'

'Well . . . a guy came in the bar Friday night, this must've been about midnight, I don't know, around then sometime.'

'Yes, go on.'

'He was pretty wound up, you know, his hands shaking and all that. He had maybe two or three drinks, I don't remember, sitting at the bar, just putting them away and looking as if . . . I don't know . . . as if somebody was *after* him or something. You know, he'd look up at the clock, and then he'd turn to look at the door, nervous, you know? Very nervous.' Martin took a deep breath. 'So Margie, being the type of person she was, being a really decent human being, she got him talking, and pretty soon he seemed more relaxed. I mean, he wasn't exactly calm, but he was more relaxed than when he came in. They talked together a long time. He didn't leave until we closed.'

'What time was that?'

'Two o'clock.'

'He left alone?'

'Yes.'

'Well, Mr Martin, how do you connect? . . .'

'He came back. It must've been about four by then, I was

still cleaning up the place. There's lots of things to do after a bar closes, you know. I usually don't get out of there till maybe five, five-thirty on a Friday night.'

'What'd he want?'

'He wanted to know Margie's last name.'

'Did you give it to him?'

'No.'

'Then ...'

'He begged me to tell him. He said he knew what it was, she'd told it to him while they were talking, but he'd forgotten it in all the excitement, and now he had to talk to her again, and would I please give him her name. I told him it was four o'clock in the morning, it was too late to talk to her. I told him to come back tomorrow, she usually stopped in after supper, he could talk to her then. So he said, No, he had to talk to her right then, and I told him to buzz off before he got me sore. I'm a pretty big guy, you know. I ... I don't like to shove my weight around, I don't think I've been in a fight since I was twelve years old, I mean it, but this guy was beginning to get on my nerves. What the hell, it was four in the morning, what did he need to talk to Margie for? I told him if he needed a broad, he was barking up the wrong tree, he should go take a walk up Culver Avenue, he'd find a hundred hookers prowling around there.' Martin paused. 'I'm sorry, I know you guys do your best, but it's the truth.'

'Go on, Mr Martin.'

'Well, that's it, I guess. He finally left.'

'What time?'

'Musta been about four-thirty.'

'But you didn't give him Mrs Ryder's last name?'

'No.'

'Or her address?'

'No, of course not.'

'What was *his* name?'

'I don't know.'

'Didn't you hear him talking?'

'I was pretty busy Friday night.'

65

'You didn't hear any of his conversation with Mrs Ryder?'

'No.'

'Do you think she really told him her name?'

'I guess so. People usually tell each other what their names are, don't they?'

'But he'd said he'd forgotten it.'

'Yes.'

'In all the excitement.'

'Yes.'

'What excitement?'

'I don't know. I guess he meant talking to her. I don't know.'

'What makes you think he finally located her?'

'Well, he might have remembered her name, and then looked up her address in the phone book. She's listed. I already checked that before I come here.'

'So you think he may have looked her up in the phone book, and then gone to her apartment?'

'Yes.'

'At four-thirty in the morning?'

'Yes.'

'To talk to her?'

'To *lay* her,' Martin said, and actually blushed.

Bert Kling had come to the apartment to make love.

It was his day off, and that was what he wanted to do. He had been thinking about it all afternoon, in fact, and had finally come over to the apartment at four-thirty, letting himself in with the key Cindy had given him long ago, and then sitting in the darkening living-room, waiting for her return.

The city outside was unwinding at day's end, dusk softening her pace, slowing her step. Kling sat in an armchair near the window, watching the sky turn blood-red and then purple and then deepening to a grape-stained silky blackness. The apartment was very still.

Somewhere out there in that city of ten million people,

66

there was a man named Walter Damascus and he had killed Mr and Mrs Andrew Leyden, had killed them brutally and viciously, pumping two shotgun blasts into each of their faces.

Kling wanted very much to go to bed with Cindy Forrest.

He did not move when he heard her key in the latch. He sat in the dark with a smile on his face, and then suddenly realized he might frighten her, and moved belatedly to turn on the table lamp. He was too late, she saw or sensed movement in the darkness. He heard her gasp, and immediately said, 'It's me, Cind'.

'Wow, you scared hell out of me,' she said, and turned on the foyer light. 'What are you doing here so early? You said . . .'

'I felt like coming over,' Kling said, and smiled.

'Yeah?'

'Mmm.'

She put her bag down on the hall table, wiggled out of her pumps, and came into the living-room.

'Don't you want a light?' she asked.

'No, it's all right.'

'Pretty out there.'

'Mmm.'

'I love that tower. See it there?'

'Yes.'

She stared through the window a moment longer, bent to kiss him fleetingly and then said, 'Make yourself a drink, why don't you?'

'You want one, too?'

'Yes. I'm exhausted,' Cindy said, and sighed, and padded softly into the bathroom. He heard the water running. He rose, turned on the lamp, and then went to where she kept her liquor in a dropleaf desk. She was out of bourbon.

'No bourbon,' he said.

'What?'

'No bourbon. You're out of bourbon,' he shouted.

'Oh, okay, I'll have a little Scotch.'

'What?' he shouted.

'Scotch,' Cindy shouted. 'A little Scotch.'

'Okay.'

'What?'

'I said *okay*.'

'Okay,' she said.

He smiled and carried the Scotch bottle into the small kitchenette. He took two short glasses down from the cabinet, poured a liberal hooker into each glass, and then nearly broke his wrist trying to dislodge the ice-cube tray from the freezer compartment. He finally chipped the accumulated frost away with a butter knife, dropped two cubes into each glass, and then carried the drinks into the bedroom. Cindy was standing at the closet in half-slip and bra, reaching for a robe. With her back to him, she said, 'I think I know what I'm going to write for my thesis, Bert'.

'What's that?' he said. 'Here's your drink.'

'Thank you,' she said. Turning, she accepted the drink and tossed her robe on to the bed. She took a long sip, said, 'Ahhh', put the glass on the dresser, and then said, 'I'll be getting my master's next June, you know. It's time I began thinking about that doctorate.'

'Um-huh,' Kling said.

'You know what I'd like to do the thesis on?' she asked, and reached behind her to unclasp her bra.

'No, what?'

'*The Detective As Voyeur*,' she said.

He thought she was kidding, of course, because as she said the words her breasts simultaneously came free of the restraining bra, and he was, in that moment, very *much* the detective as voyeur. But she stepped out of her slip and panties without so much as cracking a smile, and then went to the bed to pick up the robe and put it on. As she was belting it, she said, 'What do you think?'

'Are you serious?'

'Yes, of course,' she said, looking at him with a somewhat puzzled expression. 'Of course I'm serious. Why would I joke about something as important as my thesis?'

'Well, I don't know, I just thought . . .'

'Of *course* I'm serious,' she repeated, more strongly this time. She was frowning as she picked up her drink again. 'Why? Don't you think it's a good idea?'

'I don't know what you have in mind,' Kling said. 'You gave me the title, but ...'

'Well, I don't know if that'd be the *exact* title,' Cindy said, annoyed. She sipped some more Scotch and then said, 'Let's go into the living-room, huh?'

'Why don't we stay in here a while?' Kling said.

Cindy looked at him. He shrugged and then tried a smile.

'I'm very tired,' she said at last. 'I've had a lousy day, and I think I'm about to get my period, and I don't ...'

'All the more reason to ...'

'No, come on,' she said, and walked out of the bedroom. Kling watched her as she went. He kept watching the empty door frame long after she was out of the room. He took a swallow of his Scotch, set his jaw, and followed her into the living-room. She was sitting by the window, gazing out at the distant buildings, her bare feet propped on a hassock. 'I think it's a good idea,' she said, without turning to look at him.

'Which one?' he asked.

'My thesis,' she said testily. 'Bert, can we possibly get our minds off ...'

'*Our* minds?'

'*Your* mind,' she corrected.

'Sure,' he said.

'It isn't that I don't love you ...'

'Sure.'

'Or even that I don't *want* you ...'

'Sure.'

'It's just that at this particular moment I don't feel like making love. I feel more like crying, if you'd like to know.'

'Why?'

'I *told* you. I'm about to get my period. I always feel very depressed a day or two before.'

'Okay,' he said.

'And also, I've got my mind on this damn thesis.'

69

'Which you don't have to begin work on until next June.'

'No, not next June. I'll be getting my *master's* next June. I won't start on the doctorate till September. Anyway, what *difference* does it make, would you mind telling me? I have to start thinking about it *sometime*, don't I?'

'Yes, but ...'

'I don't know what's the matter with you today, Bert.'

'It's my day off,' he said.

'Well, *that's a non sequitur* if ever I heard one. And anyway, it hasn't been *my* day off. I went to work at nine o'clock this morning, and I interviewed twenty-four people, and I'm tired and irritable and about to get ...'

'Yes, you told me.'

'All right, so why are you picking on me?'

'Cindy,' he said, 'maybe I'd better go home.'

'Why?'

'Because I don't want to argue with you.'

'Then go home if you want to,' she said.

'All right, I will.'

'No, don't,' she said.

'Cindy ...'

'Oh, do what you want to do,' she said, 'I don't care.'

'Cindy, I love you very much,' he said. 'Now cut it out!'

'Then why don't you want to hear about my thesis?'

'I *do* want to hear about your thesis.'

'No, all you want to do is make love.'

'Well, what's wrong with that?'

'Nothing, except I don't feel like it right now.'

'Okay.'

'And you don't have to sound so damn offended, either.'

'I'm *not* offended.'

'And you could at least express a *tiny* bit of interest in my thesis. I *mean*, Bert, you can at least ask what it's going to be about.'

'What's it going to be about?' he asked.

'Go to hell, I don't feel like telling you now.'

'Okay, fine.'

'Fine,' she said.

70

They were both silent.

'Cindy,' he said at last. 'I don't even *know* you when you're like this.'

'Like what?'

'Like a bitch.'

'That's too bad, but a bitch is also part of me, I'm awfully sory. If you love me, you have to love the bitch part, too.'

'No, I *don't* have to love the bitch part,' Kling said.

'Well, don't, I don't care.'

'What's your thesis going to be about?'

'What difference does it make to you?'

'Goodnight, Cindy,' he said, 'I'm going home.'

'That's right, leave me alone when I'm feeling miserable.'

'Cindy ...'

'It's about you, you know, it was only inspired by you, you know. So go ahead and leave, what difference does it make that I love you so much and think about you day and night and even plan writing my goddamn *thesis* about you? Go ahead, go home, what do I care?'

'Oh, boy,' he said.

'Sure, oh boy.'

'Tell me about your thesis.'

'Do you *really* want to hear it?'

'Yes.'

'Well ...' Cindy said. 'I got the idea from *Blow-Up*.'

'Mmm?'

'The photographs in *Blow-Up*, you know?'

'Mmm?'

'Do you remember the part of the film where he's enlarging the black-and-white photographs, making them bigger and bigger in an attempt to figure out what happened?'

'Yes, I remember.'

'Well, it seemed to me that this entire experience was suggestive of the infantile glimpse of the primal scene.'

'The what?'

'The primal scene,' Cindy said. 'The mother and father having intercourse.'

71

'If you're going to start talking sexy,' Kling said, 'I really *am* going home.'

'I'm very serious about this, so ...'

'I'm sorry, go ahead.'

'The act of love is rarely understood by the child,' Cindy said. 'He may witness it again and again, but still remain confused about what's actually happening. The photographer in the film, you'll remember, took a great many pictures of the couple embracing and kissing in the park, do you remember that?'

'Yes, I do.'

'Which might possibly relate to the repetitive witnessing of the primal scene. The woman is young and beautiful, you remember, she was played by Vanessa Redgrave, which is how a small boy would think of his mother.'

'He would think of his mother as Vanessa Redgrave?'

'No, as young and beautiful. Bert, I swear to God, if you ...'

'All right, I'm sorry, really. Go on.'

'I'm *quite* serious, you know,' Cindy said, and took a cigarette from the inlaid box on the table beside the chair. Kling lighted it for her. 'Thank you,' she said, and blew out a stream of smoke. 'Where was I?' she asked.

'The young and beautiful mother.'

'Right, which is exactly how a small boy thinks of his mother, as young and beautiful, as the girl he wants to marry. You've heard little boys say they want to marry their mothers, haven't you?'

'Yes,' Kling said, 'I have.'

'All right, the girl in these necking-in-the-park scenes is Vanessa Redgrave, very young, very beautiful. The *man*, however, is an older man, he's got grey hair, he's obviously middle-aged. In fact, Antonioni even inserts some dialogue to that effect. I forget exactly what it was, I think the photographer says something like "A bit over the hill, isn't he?" Something like that, that's the sense of it, anyway. That this man, her lover, is a much older man. Do you understand?'

'Yes. You're saying he's a father figure.'

'Yes. Which means that those scenes in the park, when the photographer is taking pictures of the lovers, *could* be construed as a small boy watching his mother and his father making love.'

'All right.'

'Which the photographer doesn't quite understand. He's witnessing the primal scene, but he doesn't know what it's really all about. So he takes his pictures home and begins enlarging them, the way a child might enlarge upon vivid memories in an attempt to understand them. But the longer he studies the enlarged pictures, the more confused he becomes, until finally he sees what might be a pistol in one of the blow-ups. A *pistol* Bert.'

'Yes, a pistol,' he said.

'I don't have to tell you that the pistol is a fixed psychological symbol.'

'For what?'

'For what do you *think*?' Cindy asked.

'Oh,' Kling said.

'Yes. And then, to further underscore the Oedipal situation Antonioni has his photographer discover that the older man is dead, he has been *killed* – which is what every small boy wishes would happen to his father. So that he can have the mother all to himself, do you understand?'

'Yes.'

'Okay, so that's what started me thinking about the detective as a voyeur. Because, you remember, there was a great deal of suspense in that part of the movie, the part where he's blowing up the photographs. It's really a *mystery* he's working on – and he, in a very real sense, is a *detective*, isn't he?'

'Well, I suppose so.'

'Well, of course he is, Bert. The mystery element gets stronger and stronger as he continues with the investigation. And then, of course, we see an actual *corpse*. I mean, there's no question but that a murder *has* been committed. Antonioni leaves it there because he's more interested . . .'

'Leaves what? The corpse?'

73

'No, not the corpse. Well yes, he does leave the corpse there, too, as a matter of fact, but I was referring to the mystery element, I meant . . .' She suddenly looked at him suspiciously. 'Are you putting me on again?' she asked.

'Yes,' he said, and smiled.

'Well, don't be such a wise guy,' she said, and returned the smile, which he thought was at least somewhat encouraging. 'What I meant was that Antonioni doesn't pursue the *mystery* once it's served his purpose. He's doing a film about illusion and reality and alienation and all, so he's not interested in who done it or why it was done or any of that crap.'

'Okay,' Kling said. 'But I still don't see . . .'

'Well, it occurred to me that perhaps *police* investigation is similarly linked to the primitive and infantile desire to understand the primal scene.'

'Boy, that's really reaching, Cindy. How do you get . . .'

'Well, hold it a minute, will you?'

'Okay, let me hear.'

'Got you hooked, huh?' she said, and smiled again, this time *very* encouragingly, he thought.

'Go on,' he said.

'The police officer . . . the detective . . .'

'Yes?'

'. . . is privileged to see the uncensored results of violence, which is what the child *imagines* lovemaking to be. He can think his father is hurting his mother, you know, he can think her moaning is an expression of pain, he can think they're fighting. In any event, he'll often explain it to himself that way because he has neither the experience nor the knowledge to understand it in any other way. He doesn't know *what* they're doing, Bert. It's completely beyond his ken. He knows that he's stimulated by it, yes, but he doesn't know why.'

'If you think looking at a guy who's been hit with a meat axe is stimulating . . .'

'No, that's not my point. I'm not trying to make any such analogy, although I do think there's some truth to it.'

'What do you mean?'

'Well, violence *is* stimulating. Even the *results* of violence are stimulating.'

'The results of violence caused me to throw up last Saturday morning,' Kling said.

'That's stimulation of a sort, isn't it? But don't get me away from my point.'

'What *is* your point?'

'My point is ...'

'I don't think I'm going to like it.'

'Why not?'

'Because you said I inspired it.'

'Antonioni inspired it.'

'You said *I* did.'

'Not the initial impetus. *Later*, I connected it with you, which is only natural because there was a *homicide* involved, and because I'm madly in love with you and very interested in your work. All right?'

'Well, I like it a little better now, I must admit.'

'You haven't even *heard* it yet.'

'I'm waiting, I'm waiting.'

'Okay. We start with a man – the detective – viewing the results of violence and guessing at what might have happened, right?'

'Well, there's not much guesswork involved when you see two bullet holes in a guy's head. I mean, you can just possibly figure out the violent act was a shooting, you know what I mean?'

'Yes, that's obvious, but the thing you don't know is who did the shooting, or what the circumstances of the shooting were, and so on. You never know what really happened until you catch whoever did it, am I right?'

'No, you're wrong. We usually know plenty before we make an arrest. Otherwise, we don't make it. When we charge somebody, we like to think it'll stick.'

'But on what do you base your arrest?'

'On the facts. There're a lot of locked closets in criminal investigation. We open all the doors and look for skeletons.'

75

'*Exactly!*' Cindy said triumphantly. 'You search for detail. You examine each and every tiny segment of the picture in an attempt to find a clue that will make the *entire* picture more meaningful, just as the photographer did in *Blow-Up*. And very often your investigation uncovers material that's even more difficult to understand. It only becomes clear later on, the way sexual intercourse eventually becomes clear to the child when he reaches adulthood. He can then say to himself, "Oh, so *that's* what they were doing in there, they were *screwing* in there".'

'I don't recall ever having seen my mother and father doing anything like that,' Kling said.

'You've blocked it out.'

'No, I just never saw them doing anything like that.'

'Like *what*?'

'Like *that*,' Kling said.

'You can't even say the *word*,' Cindy said, and began giggling. 'You've so effectively blocked it out . . .'

'There's one thing I hate about psychologists,' Kling said.

'Yeah, what's that?' Cindy asked, still giggling.

'They're all the time analysing everything.'

'Which is exactly what *you* do every day of the week, only *you* call it investigation. Can't you see the possibilities of this, Bert?' she asked, no longer laughing, her face suddenly serious, suddenly very tired-looking again. 'Oh, I *know* I haven't really developed it yet, but don't you think it's an awfully good beginning? The detective as voyeur, the detective as privileged observer of a violent scene he can neither control nor understand, frightening by its very nature, confusing at first, but becoming more and more meaningful until it is ultimately understood. It'll make a good thesis. I don't care *what* you think.'

'*I* think it'll make a good thesis, too,' Kling said. 'Let's go work out the primal scene part of it.'

He looked down into her face just as she turned hers up, and their eyes met, and held, and neither said a word for several moments. He kept watching her, thinking how much he loved her and wanted her, and seeing the cornflower eyes edged with weariness, her face pale and drawn and drained of energy. Her lips were slightly parted, she took in a deep breath and then released it, and the hand holding the drink slowly lowered to hang limply alongside the arm of the chair. He sensed what she was about to say, Yes, she would say, Yes, she'd make love even though she didn't feel like it, even though she was depressed and tired and felt unattractive, even though she'd much rather sit here and watch the skyline and sip a little more Scotch and then doze off, even though she didn't feel the tiniest bit sexy, Yes, she would, if that was what he wanted. He read this in her eyes and perched on her lips, and he suddenly felt like a hulking rapist who had shambled up out of the sewer, so he shrugged and lightly said, 'Maybe we'd better not. Be too much like necrophilia,' and smiled. She smiled back at him, wearily and not at all encouragingly. He gently took the glass from her dangling hand and went to refill it for her.

But he was disappointed.

SIX

At eleven-thirty Wednesday morning, Anne Gilroy called the squad room and asked to talk to Kling.

'Hello,' she said, 'I hope I didn't wake you.'

'Well, no,' he said, 'I've been here for quite some time.'

'Do you remember me?' she asked.

'Yes, sure.'

'Gilroy Was Here,' she said.

'Mm-huh.'

'I thought of something,' she said.

'Oh?'

'Remember, you said if I thought of anything I should give you a call?'

'Well, actually *you* said it,' Kling said.

'That's right, I did. You have a very good memory.'

'Well,' he said, and waited.

'Don't you want to know what I thought of?'

'Is this in reference to the Leyden case?'

'Of course. You don't think I'd call you just to chat and waste your time, do you?'

'No, of course not.'

'Of course not,' Anne said, and he knew she was smiling. He was surprised, moreover, to discover that *he* was smiling, too.

'Well, what is it?' he asked. 'What did you think of?'

'I was the one who called Rose Leyden last Friday.'

'I'm sorry, I'm not following you,' he said.

'*I'm* sorry you're not following me, too,' she said, and the line went silent. 'Hello?' she said.

'Yes, I'm here.'

'Oh, good. Do you remember we got a wire from Mr

Leyden, asking the office to call his wife? About the cheque-book?'

'Oh, yes,' Kling said.

'*I* was the one who called her.'

'I see.'

'Don't you want to know what we talked about?'

'Yes, sure.'

'I can't talk right now,' Anne said.

He almost said, Then why'd you *call* right now? But he didn't. And then he wondered why he hadn't.

'When *can* you talk?' he asked instead.

'I can meet you in a half-hour,' she said. 'We can discuss it over a nice long lunch.'

'I don't take long lunches.'

'A *short* one, then. I'm very easy to get along with.'

'Even so, Miss Gilroy ...'

'Call me Anne.'

'Even so, I'm afraid I couldn't possibly meet you for lunch. Why don't I stop by at the office later today, and we can ...'

'I'll meet you for a drink at five o'clock,' she said.

The line went silent.

'I know,' she said. 'You're not allowed to drink on duty.'

'I go off duty at four forty-five,' he said, and wondered why he'd said it.

'The Roundelay Bar on Jefferson,' she said. 'Five o'clock.'

'Make it five-fifteen,' he said. 'I'll probably be coming straight from the squad room.'

'Do bring your pistol,' Anne said, and hung up.

'Who was that?' Carella asked from his desk. 'Cindy?'

'No,' Kling said, and debated lying. 'It was the Gilroy girl.'

'What'd *she* want?'

'She was the one who talked to Rose Leyden last Friday.'

'Oh? Anything?'

'I don't know. She hasn't told me what they talked about yet.'

'Why not?'

'She couldn't talk right then.'

'Then why'd she *call* right then?' Carella asked.

'To let me know.'

'Let you know *what*? She didn't tell you anything.'

'I know. I'm going to see her later. She'll fill me in then.'

'I'll just bet she will,' Carella said, and paused. 'Or vice versa,' he said, and opened the top drawer of his desk. He took his holstered .38 Detective's Special from where it rested alongside a box of cartridges, and clipped it to his belt. 'If you're interested,' he said, 'I was just talking to Pistol Permits. Nobody named Walter Damascus ever registered a .22 Iver Johnson.'

'Great,' Kling said.

'Let's go,' Carella said. 'Got to hit some of those people in the Leyden building.'

'Yeah,' Kling said, and put on his shoulder holster, and thought about Anne's parting shot, and about what Cindy had said concerning fixed psychological symbols, and was suddenly very nervous and a little scared and also a little excited. He looked at Carella sheepishly, as though his partner could read his mind, and then followed him out of the squad room.

Mrs Carmen Leibowitz was a widow in her middle fifties, a chic woman with an agreeable and cooperative manner. She lived directly across the hall from the Leydens and was of course shocked, and not a little frightened, by what had happened. The neighbours were getting up a petition, she told the detectives, asking for better protection in the building. It was terrible the way the neighbourhood was deteriorating, people getting killed and robbed in elevators and in their own beds, absolutely frightening. She had been living in the same building for thirty-four years now, had come here as a young bride, had raised a family here, had continued living here even after her husband's fatal coronary more than three years ago. But it had never been like this, with animals waiting to stab you or shoot you, she was afraid of going downstairs any more.

'I'm a woman living alone,' she told them. 'It's very difficult for a woman living alone.'

She spoke in a very loud and somewhat grating voice, sitting on a well-worn Louis XVI settee against a panelled wall in a living-room hung with oil paintings. She was wearing a Chanel suit, and Henri Bendel pumps, her hair meticulously coiffed, her make-up impeccable : she told the detectives they'd caught her on her way downtown to do some shopping. Carella promised they would not delay her long, and then declined her offer of coffee and raisin cake. In the kitchen, they could hear someone puttering around, dishes and silverware clinking.

'Who's that?' Carella asked, and gestured towards the kitchen.

Mrs Leibowitz, watching his face intently, said, 'My girl'.

'Your daughter?'

Still studying his face, she said, 'No, no, my maid'.

'Oh,' Carella said.

'Does she sleep in?' Kling asked.

'No,' Mrs Leibowitz answered. She had given his face that same intense scrutiny, and she continued to gaze at him now, as though waiting for him to say something more. When it became apparent that he was not going to speak, she turned back to Carella, studying him with an identical attitude of concentrated expectancy.

'What time does she come in?' Carella asked.

'Nine in the morning. Except Thursdays and Sundays.'

'And what time does she leave?'

'After dinner. She does the dishes and goes.'

Carella turned towards Kling and said, 'That means she wouldn't have been here on the morning the murders were committed. It'd have been too early for her.'

He turned back towards Mrs Leibowitz, who smiled, said, 'Mmmm', nodded, and then fastened her eyes to his face again. There was something terribly familiar about her scrutiny. It made Carella uncomfortable, creating a vague and elusive aura of *déjà vu*, the certain knowledge that he had been looked at in this same way by this same woman many many times before. And yet he knew he had never met her before this morning. Frowning, he said, 'Were *you* at home on the morning of the murders, Mrs Leibowitz?'

'Yes, I was,' she said.

'Did you hear anything across the hall?' he asked.

'I'm a very heavy sleeper,' she said.

'These would have been shotgun blasts,' Kling said, and she turned towards him and smiled. '*Four* of them,' he continued. 'They would have been very loud.'

'The shots, do you mean?' she asked.

'Yes,' Kling said, and frowned. 'The shotgun blasts.'

'I was asleep,' Mrs Leibowitz said. 'The newspapers said it happened in the middle of the night. I was asleep.'

'These shots would have been loud enough to have wakened you,' Carella said.

She turned to him, and did not answer.

'But you slept through them,' he said.

Studying his face, she said, 'Yes. I slept through them'.

'We figure the murders took place some time between three-thirty and four-thirty,' Carella said, 'about that time. Would you remember? ...'

'I'm *sure* I was asleep,' Mrs Leibowitz said, watching him.

'And heard nothing?'

'I'm a very heavy sleeper,' she said again, and waited, watching Carella's face. He suddenly knew *what* she was watching, suddenly knew why her expression looked so familiar. He rose abruptly, turning his back to her, walking from the settee and saying in a normal speaking voice, 'I think you're hard of hearing, Mrs Leibowitz, am I right?' and then turned immediately, and looked at her, and saw that she was smiling and watching him, still waiting expectantly for him to speak.

His wife Teddy was a deaf mute.

He had lived with her for a long long time now, and he knew the look that came over her face, knew the intense concentration in her eyes whenever she 'listened' to him, whenever she read his lips or his hands. That same expression was on Mrs Leibowitz's face now as she waited for him to speak again. The part of his face she studied so intently was his mouth.

'Mrs Leibowitz,' he said gently, 'who else lives on this floor?'

'There are only three apartments on the floor,' she said.

'Who's in the third one?' Kling asked.

She turned quickly at the sound of his voice, but did not answer him. Kling glanced at Carella.

'The third apartment,' Carella said gently. 'Who's in it, Mrs Leibowitz?'

'A family named Pimm. Mr and Mrs George Pimm. They're not here now.'

'Where are they?'

'In Puerto Rico.'

'On vacation?'

'Vacation, yes,' she said.

She really carries it off very well, Carella thought. So long as she's facing you, she can read your lips like an expert, even Teddy misses a word every now and then, but not Carmen Leibowitz, who fixes you with those very blue eyes of hers, clamps them to your lips and refuses to let go until she has wrung from them the meaning of their movement, but only when she's facing you. If she turns away, she misses the sense completely, probably hearing only a faint rumble that causes her to turn towards the speaker. She's developed a lovely smile and a faint encouraging nod and a look of patient empathy, and she pulls off her deception really quite well because it would not do to wear a hearing aid, a hearing aid would not look good on a woman so chic, a woman so well-groomed. I wish she could meet Teddy, he thought. I wish she could meet my wonderful wife, who is as deaf and as mute as a sunrise.

'When did they leave?' he asked, taking pains to face her directly and to exaggerate each word.

'A week ago Sunday.'

'Then they were gone before the murders?'

'Yes, before.'

'When will they be back, do you know?'

'George said two weeks, I think. I'm not sure.'

'That would be . . .' he started, inadvertently turning towards Kling, and then immediately correcting his oversight, and turning back to find Mrs Leibowitz sitting with that same painfully expectant smile on her face, not having heard a word he'd said. 'That would be next Sunday,' Carella said.

'Yes,' she answered. She knew now that he knew, but she sat in unshakeable confidence that she could continue to deceive, or perhaps only confidence that he would *allow* her to deceive.

'So with the Pimms gone,' he said, 'you'd have been the only person on this floor. And you of course were asleep.'

'Yes,' she said.

'Well, then, I guess there's nothing further to ask,' he said. 'Thank you very much.'

'Thank *you*,' she said, and showed them to the door.

They talked to everyone in the building that afternoon, hoping to find someone who might have been awakened by the shots, someone who might have gone to the window and looked outside, seen a car downstairs perhaps, a yellow Buick perhaps, read a licence number and remembered it.

Seven people admitted they had heard the shots. Two of them said they figured it was a truck downstairs, the backfire cliché apparently having been pounded into the unconscious of the average man as a reasonable explanation for any loud and sudden noise. A man on the fourth floor said he had got out of bed when he heard the first explosions . . .

'Two of them?' Carella asked.

'Yes, two, and very loud. I got out of bed and then heard someone yelling . . .'

'A man or a woman?'

'Hard to tell, just somebody yelling, you know, and then two more explosions, also very loud.'

'What did you do?' Carella asked.

'I went back to bed,' the man said.

A woman on the ninth floor had heard the shots only distantly, and had been frightened by them, and had stayed in bed for a full five minutes before going to the window to investigate. She had seen a car pulling away from the kerb.

'What kind of a car?' Carella asked.

'I don't know. I can't tell makes.'

'What colour was it?'

'A dark colour.'

'Not yellow?'

'No. Oh, no. Definitely not yellow.'

'Did you see the licence plate?'

'No, I'm sorry. I didn't.'

The remaining three people said they had known immediately that the noise was gunfire. They also said they'd thought it had come from the street, but none of them had gone to the window for a look outside, nor had any of them thought of telephoning the police. Par for the course, Carella thought, and thanked them, and wearily trudged downstairs with Kling.

'So what do you think?' he asked.

'The car pulling away could have been anybody,' Kling said. 'Couple of kids necking, guy going to work, anybody.'

'Or maybe Walter Damascus.'

'His girlfriend drives a yellow Buick.'

'Sure, but what does *he* drive?'

'*Nothing* is my guess. Otherwise, why would he need her to pick him up?'

'It doesn't seem possible, does it?' Carella said.

'*What* doesn't?'

'That a guy could vanish into thin air this way. We know his name, we know where he lives, we've got his fingerprints, we've even got a good description of him. The only thing we haven't got is *him*.'

'Maybe we'll get lucky,' Kling said.

'When?' Carella asked.

*　　　*　　　*

The Roundelay Bar was on Jefferson Avenue, three blocks from the new museum. At five-fifteen that afternoon, when Kling arrived for his business meeting with Anne Gilroy, it was thronged with advertising executives and pretty young secretaries and models, all of whom behaved like guests at a private cocktail party, moving, drinking, chattering, moving on again, hardly any of them sitting at the handful of tables scattered throughout the dimly lit room.

Anne Gilroy was sitting at a table in the far corner, wearing an open crochet dress over what appeared to be a body stocking. At least, Kling *hoped* it was a body stocking, and not just a body. He felt very much out of place in an atmosphere as sleek and as sophisticated as this one, where everyone seemed to be talking about the latest Doyle Dane campaign, or the big Solters and Sabinson coup, or the new Blaine Thompson three-sheet, whatever any of those were. He felt shabbily dressed in his blue plaid jacket, his tie all wrong and improperly knotted, his gun in its shoulder holster causing a very un-Chipplike bulge, felt in fact like a bumbling country hick who had inadvertently stumbled into whatever was making this city tick. And besides, he felt guilty as hell.

Anne waved the moment she saw him. He moved his way through the buzzing crowd and then sat beside her and looked around quickly, certain somehow that Cindy would be standing behind one of the pillars, brandishing a hatchet.

'You're right on time,' Anne said, smiling. 'I like punctual men.'

'Have you ordered yet?' he asked.

'No, I was waiting for you.'

'Well, what would you like?'

'Martinis give me a loose, free feeling,' she said. 'I'll have a martini. Straight up.'

He signalled to the waiter and ordered a martini for her and a Scotch and water for himself.

'Do you like my dress?' Anne asked.

'Yes, it's very pretty.'

'Did you think it was me?'

'What do you mean?'

'Underneath.'

'I wasn't sure.'

'It isn't.'

'Okay.'

'Is something wrong?' she asked.

'No, no. No. No.'

'You keep looking around the room.'

'Habit. Check it out, you know, known criminals, you know, types. Occupational hazard.'

'My, you're nervous,' she said. 'Does my dress make you nervous?'

'No, it's a very nice dress.'

'I wish I had the guts to *really* wear it naked underneath,' Anne said, and giggled.

'Well, you'd get arrested,' Kling said. 'Section 1140 of the Penal Law.'

'What do you mean?'

'Exposure of person,' Kling said, and began quoting. 'A person who wilfully and lewdly exposes his person, or the private parts thereof, in any public place, or in any place where others are present, or procures another so to expose himself, is guilty of a misdemeanour.'

'Oh, my,' Anne said.

'Yes,' Kling said, suddenly embarrassed.

' "Private parts", I love that.'

'Well, that's what we call them. I mean, in police work. I mean, that's the way we refer to them.'

'Yes, I love it.'

'Mmm,' Kling said. 'Hey, here're the drinks.'

'Shall I mix it, sir?' the waiter asked.

'What?'

'Did you want this mixed, sir?'

'Oh. Yes. Yes, just a little water in it, please,' he said, and smiled at Anne and almost knocked over her martini. The waiter poured a little water into the Scotch and moved away.

'Cheers,' Kling said.

'Cheers,' Anne said, 'do you have a girlfriend?'

Kling, who was already drinking, almost choked. 'What?' he cried.

'A girlfriend.'

'Yes,' he answered glumly, and nodded.

'Is that why you're so worried?'

'Who's worried?' he said.

'You shouldn't be,' Anne said. 'After all, this is only a business meeting.'

'That's right. I'm not worried at all,' Kling said.

'What's she like? Your girlfriend?' Anne said.

'Well, I'd much rather discuss the conversation you had with Mrs Leyden.'

'Are you engaged?'

'Not officially.'

'What does *that* mean?'

'It means we plan on getting married someday, I guess, but we ...'

'You *guess*?'

'Well, no, actually there's no guesswork involved. We simply haven't set the date, that's all. Cindy's still in school, and ...'

'Is that her name? Cindy?'

'Yes. For Cynthia.'

'And you say she's still in school? How old is she?'

'Twenty-three. She's finishing her master's this June.'

'Oh.'

'Yes, and she'll be going on for her doctorate in the fall.'

'Oh.'

'Yes,' Kling said.

'She must be very bright.'

'She is.'

'I barely finished high school,' Anne said, and paused. 'Is she pretty?'

'Yes.' Kling took another swallow of Scotch and then said, '*I'm* supposed to be the detective, but *you're* asking all the questions.'

'I'm a very curious girl,' Anne said, and smiled. 'But go ahead. What do you want to know?'

'What time did you call Mrs Leyden last Friday?'

'Oh, I thought you were going to ask some questions about *me*.'

'No, actually I ...'

'I'm twenty-five years old,' Anne said, 'born and raised right here in the city. My father's a Transit Authority employee, my mother's a housewife. We're all very Irish.' She paused and sipped at the martini. 'I began working for AT & M right after I graduated high school, and I've been there since. I believe in making love not war, and I think you're possibly the handsomest man I've ever met in my life.'

'Thank you,' Kling mumbled, and hastily lifted his glass to his lips.

'Does that embarrass you?'

'No.'

'What *does* it do?'

'I'm not sure.'

'I believe in speaking honestly and frankly,' Anne said.

'I see that.'

'Would you like to go to bed with me?'

Kling did not answer immediately, because what popped into his mind instantly was the single word *Yes!* and it was followed by a succession of wild images interspersed with blinking neon lights that spelled out additional messages such as *You're goddamn right I'd like to go to bed with you* and *When?* and *Your place or mine?* and things like that. So he waited until he had regained control of his libido, and then he calmly said, 'I'll have to think it over. In the meantime, let's talk about Mrs Leyden, shall we?'

'Sure,' Anne said. 'What would you like to know?'

'What time did you call her?'

'Just before closing time Friday.'

'Which *was*?'

'About ten to five, something like that.'

'Do you remember the conversation?'

'Yes. I said, "Hello, may I please speak to Mrs Leyden?" and she said, "*This* is Mrs Leyden". So I informed her that her husband had wired us from California to ask that she send him a fresh chequebook, and she said she knew all about it, but thanks anyway.'

'She knew all about *what*?'

'The chequebook.'

'How'd she know?'

'She said her husband had called from the Coast that morning to say he'd be in San Francisco all weekend, and that he'd be moving on to Portland on Monday morning and wanted her to send a fresh chequebook to the Logan Hotel there.'

'What time had he called her?'

'She didn't say.'

'But if he'd already called her, why'd he bother sending a wire to the company?'

'I don't know. Just double-checking, I guess.'

'I wonder if he called her again later to say he'd be coming home instead?'

'She didn't mention getting two calls.'

'This was close to five, you said?'

'Yes, just before closing.'

'Was he normally so careful?'

'What do you mean?'

'Would he normally make a call and then back it with a wire asking the company to convey the identical information?'

'He may have sent the wire *before* he called his wife.'

'Even so.'

'Besides, the company paid his expenses, so why not?' Anne smiled. 'Have you thought it over yet?' she asked.

'No, not yet.'

'Think about it. I'd like to. Very much.'

'Why?'

'Because you're stunning.'

'Oh, come on,' Kling said.

'You *are*. I'm not easily impressed, believe me. I think I'm in love with you.'

'That's impossible.'

'No, it isn't.'

'Sure it is. A person can't just fall in love with a person without knowing anything about the person. That only happens in the movies.'

'I know everything there is to know about you,' Anne said. 'Let's have another drink, shall we?'

'Sure,' Kling said, and signalled the waiter. 'Another round,' he said when the waiter came over, and then turned to Anne, who was watching with her eyes wide and her cheeks flushed, and he suddenly thought, Jesus, I think she really *is* in love with me. 'Anyway, as you said, this is a business meeting, and ...'

'It's a lot more than that,' Anne said, 'and you *know* it. I think you knew it when you agreed to meet me, but if you didn't know it then, you certainly know it now. I love you and I want to go to bed with you. Let's go to my apartment right this minute.'

'Hold it, hold it,' Kling said, thinking. What am I, crazy? Say Yes. Pay the check and get out of here, take this luscious little girl to wherever she wants to go, hurry up before she changes her mind. 'You don't know me at al,' he said, 'really. We've hardly even *talked* to each other.'

'What's there to talk about? You're a wonderfully good-looking man, and you're undoubtedly brave because you *have* to be brave in your line of work, and you're idealistic because otherwise why would you be involved in crime prevention, and you're bright as hell, and I think it's very cute the way you're so embarrassed because I'm begging you to take me to bed. There's nothing else I have to know, do you have a mole on your thigh, or something?'

'No,' he said, and smiled.

'So?'

'Well, I ... I can't right now, anyway.'

'Why not?' Anne paused, and then moved closer to him,

91

covering his hand with hers on the table top. 'Bert,' she whispered, 'I love you and I want you.'

'Listen,' he said, 'let's uh think this over a little, huh? I'm uh ...'

'Don't *you* want *me*?'

'Yes, but ...'

'Ah, one for our side,' she said, and smiled. 'What is it, then?'

'I'm uh engaged,' he said. 'I already told you that.'

'So what?'

'Well, you uh wouldn't want me to ...'

'Yes, I would,' Anne said.

'Well, I couldn't. Not now, I mean, maybe not ever.'

'My telephone number is Washington 6–3841. Call me later tonight, after you leave your girlfriend.'

'I'm not seeing her tonight.'

'You're *not*?' Anne asked astonished.

'No. She goes to school on Wednesday nights.'

'Then, that settles it,' Anne said. 'Pay the check.'

'I'll pay the check,' Kling said, 'but nothing's settled.'

'You're coming with me,' Anne said. 'We're going to make love six times, and then I'm going to cook you some dinner, and then we'll make love another six times. What time do you have to be at work tomorrow morning?'

'The answer is no,' Kling said.

'Okay,' Anne said breezily. 'But write down the telephone number.'

'I don't have to write it down.'

'Oh, such a smart cop,' Anne said. 'What's the number?'

'Washington 6–3841.'

'You'll call me,' she said. 'You'll call me later tonight when you think of me all alone in my bed, pining away for you.'

'I don't think so,' he said.

'Maybe not tonight,' she amended. 'But soon.'

'I can't promise that.'

'Anyway,' she said, 'it doesn't matter. Because if *you* don't call *me*, *I'll* call *you*. I have no pride, Bert. I want you, and I'm going to get you. Consider yourself forewarned.'

'You scare hell out of me,' he said honestly.

'Good. Do I also excite you just a little bit?'

'Yes,' he said, and smiled. 'Just a little bit.'

'That's *two* for our side,' she said, and squeezed his hand.

SEVEN

THURSDAY WAS Halloween, so naturally nothing happened on either case. That's because on Halloween there are ghouls and goblins and witches and spooks stirring on the sweet October air, and they put a hex on anybody trying to do good. The detectives of the 87th were trying to do good by solving those several murders, but it was no use, not on Halloween. So both cases sat right where they were. Besides, there was plenty of other mischief to take care of on that Thursday, October 31st.

Carella knew, of course, that Halloween was in reality the day before All Saints' Day, a church festival celebrated on November 1st each year in honour of all the saints. He further knew that All Saints' Day was sometimes called Allhallows (*hallow* meaning *saint*), and Halloween, before it got bastardized, was originally called Allhallows Even (*even* being another way of saying *eve*), and even *even* became contracted to *e'en*, hence Hallowe'en, and finally everybody dropped the apostrophe and it became Halloween, a long way from Allhallows Even perhaps, but that's the way the witch's brew bubbles, bubeluh.

To Carella, Allhallows Even sounded a great deal more pious than Halloween, but pious was the *last* thing Halloween had become in America. So perhaps the bastardized and contracted handle was really quite descriptive of an unofficial holiday that had evolved over the years into an excuse for malicious mischief across the length and breadth of the nation. The mischief had been present when Carella was a boy too, but it all seemed far more innocent in those days. In those days he would roam the October streets wearing a fleece-lined pseudo-World War I leather aviator's helmet with goggles, carrying either a piece of coloured chalk

94

(or white chalk, for that matter, though coloured chalk was far more desirable); or else a stick stripped from an orange crate the end of which had been chalked; or else a sock full of flour. The idea was to chase a person, preferably a girl, and either chalk a line down her back, or slap her with the stick, thereby chalking her back, or hit her with a sock full of flour, which also left a mark on her back. You then shouted 'Halloween!' and ran like hell, usually giggling. The girl giggled too. Everybody giggled. It was good clean fun, or so it seemed in Carella's memory. At night, the kids would build an enormous bonfire in the middle of the city street, tossing into it wood scavenged from empty lots, old furniture and crates begged from apartment-building super-intendents during the long, exciting day. The flames would leap skyward, shooting sparks and cinders, the boys would run into the street like hobgoblins themselves, to throw more fuel on to the fire, and then the collection of wood exhausted itself and the flames dwindled, and the girls all went upstairs while the boys stood around the smouldering fire and peed on it.

That was Halloween, Carella thought.

Today ...

Well, today, for example, two kids had broken the plate-glass window of a bakery shop on Ainsley Avenue because the owner had refused to give them money for UNICEF. They had gone into the shop carrying their orange-and-black milk containers with the UNICEF wrappers and asked the man to contribute to the relief fund and the man had said, get the hell out of my shop. So they had gone out of his shop and hurled two bricks through his window be-sides, executing the trick because they'd been refused the treat. Now, surely there was something insane about smash-ing a man's window because he refused to contribute to the welfare of starving children all over the world, something almost as insane as fighting wars to preserve peace. It seemed to Carella that a man accused of assault could not reasonably offer as his defence the statement, 'I punched him in the nose because I wanted to prevent a fight'. This

95

was no more reasonable than smashing a plate-glass window costing five hundred dollars merely because some bastard had refused to contribute a nickel to a worthwhile cause. With this sort of reasoning afoot, even on Halloween when *all* reason was distorted, the lunatics were well on their way to taking over the asylum.

Other 'mischievous' happenings that day seemed to confirm the uprising of the inmates.

Six boys, inspired by the thought that this was Halloween – and anything goes on Halloween because boys will be boys and what's wrong with letting go once a year – six boys dragged a twelve-year-old girl into an alley and raped her one after the other because she was carrying a shopping bag full of Halloween treats which she refused to share with them. The boys ranged in age from sixteen to eighteen, and none of them would have given a seventh-grade girl a glance had this not been the day of the year when the banshees were supposed to howl.

Over on South Eleventh, a high-school senior shoved her classmate off the roof because she insisted on chalking 'Irene Loves Pete' in a heart on the roof's brick parapet. Irene explained to the police that she did *not* love Pete, she really loved Joey, and she had pleaded with her friend not to write such libel on the wall, but her friend had insisted, so she had shoved her over the low parapet. She could not explain why she had shouted 'Halloween!' as her friend plummeted the seven storeys to the pavement below.

On Culver Avenue, a grown-up man chasing a fifteen-year-old boy who had sprayed shaving cream on to the windows of his parked automobile, only happened to knock down a woman wheeling a baby carriage, which baby carriage and its four-month-old occupant rolled into the street to be squashed flat by an oncoming milk truck. The man told the police that he was of course sorry about the accident, but why didn't they do something about all this rampant vandalism?

On The Stem, near Twentieth Street, two enterprising professionals entered a delicatessen wearing rubber Halloween masks, shouted 'Trick or treat!' at the owner of the place, and promptly stuck loaded revolvers across the counter. The owner, imbued with a bit of Halloween spirit himself, threw a pound and a half of pastrami at one of the men and then stabbed the other with a very sharp carving knife that entered his throat just where the rubber mask ended. The second man, his mask and his coat dripping very good lean pastrami, fired at the owner and left him dead, and a kid running past the shop did a little excited jig in the doorway and chanted, 'Halloween, Halloween, Halloween'.

It was a great little holiday, Halloween.

Cops just loved it.

Nevertheless, at six o'clock on Allhallows Even, after a tiring day of inactivity on the Leyden case and all sorts of activity in the streets preventing and discouraging mayhem, not to mention arresting people here and there who had allowed their celebration to become a bit too uninhibited, Steve Carella watched his wife as she painted the face of his son, and prepared to go out into the streets once again.

'I got a great idea, Pop,' Mark said. He was the oldest of the twins by seven minutes, which gave him seniority as well as masculine superiority over his sister April. It was Mark who generally had the 'great' ideas and April who invariably put him down with something sweet like, 'That's the stupidest idea I ever heard in my life'.

'What's your idea?' Carella asked.

'I think we should go to Mr Oberman's house . . .'

'Oberman the Creep,' April observed.

'That's not a nice way to talk about an old man,' Carella said.

'But he *is* a creep, Daddy.'

'That doesn't matter,' Carella said.

'Anyway,' Mark said, 'I think we should go to his house, and April and me'll knock on the door . . .'

'April and *I*,' Carella corrected.

Mark looked up at his father, wondering whether he should try to joke about, 'Oh, are *you* going to knock on the door, too?' and decided in his infinite wisdom that he'd better not risk it, even though it had gone over pretty well once with Miss Rutherford, who taught the third grade at the local elementary school. 'April and *I*,' he said, and smiled at his father angelically, and then beamed at his mother as she continued drawing a black moustache under his nose, and then said, 'April and I will knock on Mr Oberman's door and yell, "Trick or treat", and when he opens it, you stick your gun in his face.'

Teddy, who was watching her son's lips as he talked, shook her head violently, and looked up at her husband. Before Carella could answer, April said, 'That's the stupidest idea I ever heard in my life', her life to date having consisted of eight years, four months, and ten days.

Mark said, 'Shut up, who asked *you*?' and Teddy scowled at her husband, warning him to put an end to this before it got out of hand, and then grasping both of Mark's shoulders to turn him towards her so that she could properly finish the job. She was using felt-tipped watercolour markers, and whereas her make-up artistry might not have passed muster with the National Repertory, it looked pretty good to her from where she knelt beside her son. She had enlarged and angled Mark's eyebrows with the black marker, and had then used green eyeshadow on his lids, and the black marker again to draw a sinister, drooping moustache and an evil-looking goatee. Her son was supposed to be Dracula, who did not have either a moustache or a beard, but she felt he looked far too cherubic without them, and had taken artistic licence with the Bram Stoker character. She was now using the bright-red marker to paint in a few drops of blood under his lip, and since her back was to Carella, she did not hear him admonish Mark first for his idiotic idea about brandishing a real gun, and next for yelling at his sister. She dotted a last tiny dribble of blood below the other three larger drops, and then rose and stepped back to admire her handiwork.

'How do I look?' Mark asked Carella.

'Horrible.'

'Great!' Mark shouted, and ran out of the room to search for a mirror.

'Make me pretty, Mommy,' April said, looking directly up at her mother. Teddy smiled, and then slowly and carefully moved her fingers in the universal language of the deaf mute while Carella and the little girl watched.

'She says she doesn't *have* to make you pretty,' Carella said. 'You *are* pretty.'

'I could read almost all of it,' April said, and hugged Teddy fiercely. 'I'm the Good Princess, you know,' she said to her father.

'That's true, you *are* the Good Princess.'

'Are there *bad* princesses, too?'

Teddy was replacing the caps on the felt-tipped markers to keep them from drying out. She smiled at her daughter, shook her head, reached into her purse for a lipstick tube, and then carried it to where April waited patiently for the touches that would transform her into a true good princess. Kneeling before her, Teddy expertly began to apply the lipstick. The two looked remarkably alike, the same brown eyes and black hair, the clearly defined widow's peak, the long lashes and generous mouth. April wore a long gown and cape fashioned of hunter-green velvet by Fanny, their housekeeper. Teddy wore tight blue jeans and a white tee shirt, her hair falling on to her cheek now as she bent her head, concentrating on the line of April's mouth. She touched her fingertip to the lipstick and brushed a bit of it on to each of April's cheeks, blending it, and then reached for the eyeshadow she had used on her son, using it more subtly on April's lids, mindful of the fact that her daughter was not supposed to be a blood-thirsty vampire. Using a mascara brush, she darkened April's lashes and then turned her to face Carella.

'Beautiful,' Carella said. 'Go look at yourself.'

'Am I, Mommy?' April asked and, without waiting for an affirming nod, scurried out of the room.

Fanny came in not a moment later, grinning.

'There's a horrid little beast rushing all about the kitchen

99

with blood dripping from his mouth,' she said, and then, pretending to notice Carella for the first time even though he'd been home for more than half an hour, added, 'Well it's himself. And will you be taking the children out for their mischief?'

'I will,' Carella said.

'Mind you're back at seven, because that's when the roast'll be done.'

'I'll be back by seven,' Carella promised. To Teddy, he said, 'I thought you said there were no bad princesses'.

'And what is *that* supposed to mean?' Fanny asked.

She had come to the Carellas more than eight years ago as a one-month gift from Teddy's father, who had felt his daughter needed at least that much time to rearrange the household after the birth of twins. In those days Fanny's hair was blue, and she wore a pince-nez, and she weighed a hundred and fifty pounds. The prepaid month had gone by all too quickly, and Carella had regretfully informed her that he could not afford a full-time housekeeper on his meagre salary. But Fanny was an indomitable broad who had never had a family of her own, and who rather liked this one. So she told Carella he could pay her whatever he might scrape up for the time being, and she would supplement her income with night jobs, she being a trained nurse and a very strong healthy woman to boot. Carella had flatly refused, and Fanny had put her hands on her hips and said, 'Are you going to throw me out into the street, is that it?' and they had argued back and forth, and Fanny had stayed. She was still with them. Her hair was now bleached red, and she wore harlequin glasses with black frames, and her weight was down to a hundred and forty as a result of chasing after two very lively children. Her influence on the family unit was perhaps best reflected in the speech of the twins. As infants, they'd been alone with her and their mother for much of the day, and since Teddy could not utter a word, much of their language had been patterned after Fanny's. It was not unusual to hear Mark referring to someone as a lace-curtain shanty Irish son of a B, or little

April telling a playmate to go scratch her arse. It made life colourful, to say the least.

Fanny stood now with her hands on her ample hips, daring Carella to explain what he had meant by his last remark. Carella fixed her with a menacing detective-type stare and said, 'I was referring, dear, to the fact that you are sometimes overbearing and raucous and could conceivably be thought of as a *bad* princess, *that* is what it's supposed to mean', and Fanny burst out laughing.

'How can you live with such a beast?' she asked Teddy, still laughing, and then went out of the room, wagging her head.

'Daddy, are you coming?' Mark shouted.

'Yes, son,' he answered.

He folded Teddy into his arms and kissed her. Then he went out into the living-room and took the children one by each hand, and went out into the streets to ring doorbells with them. He almost forgot, but not quite, that he had seen a seventeen-year-old girl squashed flat on the pavement today because she had scrawled 'Irene Loves Pete' into a heart on the brick parapet of a roof.

The call to the squad room came at 9.45 PM.

Meyer Meyer, who was alone and catching, picked up the receiver and said, '87th Squad, Detective Meyer'.

'This is Patrolman Breach,' the voice said, 'Benny Breach.'

'Yeah, Benny?'

'I figured I'd better call this one in. I was passing a bar on Culver and the owner of the place stopped me and asked me to come inside.'

'Yeah?'

'Yeah, so I went in and there's a guy standing on one of the tables and saying all sorts of crazy things.'

'Like what, Benny?'

'Like he said he killed some dame.'

The guy who had said he'd killed a girl was a huge man, six

feet five inches tall and weighing more than two hundred pounds. His nose was massive, his cheekbones high with an angled, chiselled look, his mouth wide, his chin rough-hewn. When he came into the squad room with Patrolman Breach, he was still reeling a bit from the effects of all the alcohol he'd consumed.

'What is the matter here in this city,' he asked, his words slurred, 'when a man can't have a few little drinks without the police picking him up like this in this city?'

'He's been drinking pretty heavy, sir,' Breach said.

'Yeah,' Meyer answered. 'See if there's any coffee in the Clerical Office, will you?'

'Yes, sir,' Breach said, and went down the corridor.

'I am not drunk,' the man said.

'What's your name?' Meyer asked.

'That is *my* business.'

'All right, if you're not drunk, then please listen to what I'm going to say now, because it can be important to you.'

'I'm listening,' the man said.

'In keeping with the Supreme Court decision of 1966 in the case of Miranda versus Arizona, I'm required to advise you of your rights, and that's what I'm doing now.'

'Fine,' the man said.

'First, you have the right to remain silent if you choose, do you understand that?'

'Absolutely.'

'Do you also understand that you do not have to answer any police questions?'

'Oh, sure.'

'And do you understand that if you do answer questions, your answers may be used as evidence against you?'

'Yep, yep. Yep.'

'You have the right to consult with an attorney before or during police questioning, do you understand that?'

'Perfect, perfect.'

'And if you decide to exercise that right but do not have the funds with which to hire counsel, you are entitled to have a lawyer appointed without cost, to consult with him before or during questioning. Have you got that?'

'Got it. Right on the button.'

'Do you understand all of your rights as I've just explained them to you?'

'No, I don't,' the man answered, and grinned drunkenly.

Meyer sighed. 'Breach,' he said, 'are you getting that coffee?'

'Coming!' Breach called.

In the silence of the squad room, they gave the man three cups of coffee to drink, and when Meyer was sure he was reasonably sober, he went through the entire Miranda-Escobedo bit again, and ended his warnings by saying, 'Are you willing to answer questions without the presence of an attorney?'

'What?'

'Do you want a lawyer or don't you?'

'Why do I need a lawyer?'

'That's for you to decide. Are you willing to answer questions without one?'

'I am,' the man said.

'All right, what's your name?'

'I refuse to answer that question.'

'Why?'

'Because I don't want my mother to know I've been inside a police station.'

'Why? Are you afraid she'll find out why we brought you here?'

'Why *did* you bring me here?'

'Don't you know?'

'Because I was drunk?'

'No, that's not the reason.'

'Then that *is* the reason? I didn't do anything wrong.'

'Do you remember what you said in the bar?'

'No.'

'Do you remember getting up on one of the tables and making an announcement to everyone in the bar?'

'No.'

'Patrolman Breach, would you tell this man what he said?'

Breach looked embarrassed for a moment. He shrugged, and then said, 'Mister, you got up on one of the tables and said you killed some girl'.

'I never said anything like that.'

'Yes, you did. You were saying it to everybody in the bar even before I come in. By the time I got there, you were up on one of the tables waving your drinks around and telling everybody you'd killed a girl and got away with it.'

'No.'

'Well, that's what you said,' Breach insisted.

'I was drunk. If I said anything like that, I must have made it up.'

'You never killed anybody, is that right?' Meyer asked.

'Never.'

'Then why'd you make up such a thing?'

'I don't know.'

'You must have realized somebody would call the police.'

'Well, I was drunk,' the man said.

He had a polite, shy manner about him now that he was sober. Looking at him, Meyer saw that his immense hands were brown and calloused, like a farmer's.

'Do you live here in the city, sir?' he asked.

'No, I don't.'

'Where do you live?'

'Is there any more of that coffee?'

'Breach?'

'I'll get some,' Breach said.

'Where *do* you live?' Meyer repeated.

'Upstate.'

'Where?'

'Carey. It's near Huddleston. On route 190, the turnoff just before the road to Mount Torrance.'

'What are you doing here in the city?' Meyer asked.

'Just down for a few days.'

'On business or pleasure?'

'Business mostly.'

'What's your business?'

'Woodenware. We've got a little shop up home, and we make coffee tables, bowls, spoons, things like that. Out of wood. I come into the city every so often to sell it.'

'When were you here last?'

'Oh, I guess it was April sometime.'

'When did you get to the city this time?'

'Last Thursday.'

'Mmm-huh,' Meyer said. 'What about this girl you killed?'

'I didn't kill any girl.'

'Who *did* you kill?'

'Nobody.'

'You said you killed a girl.'

'I said it when I was drunk. *If* I said it.'

'What's your name, mister?'

'I'd rather not say.'

'We can find out, you know.'

'Then find out.'

'Look, mister, you'd better start levelling with me, because I can tell you this is a pretty serious matter here. A woman was found dead in her apartment about a mile from where we picked you up tonight, and indications are that she was killed last Friday night sometime. Now, suppose you tell me just where you were at that time?'

'When you were telling me my rights you said I didn't have to answer any questions if I didn't want to.'

'That's what I said.'

The man paused. 'All right,' he said, 'I don't want to answer any more questions,' and that was when Cotton Hawes walked into the squad room.

'A madhouse out there,' he said to Meyer, 'gets worse every goddamn year.' He glanced at the man, turned away from him, turned back to him again, and then said, 'Don't I know you?'

'I don't think so,' the man said.

'Sure, I do,' Hawes said, and walked closer to the desk and peered into his face, frowning, trying to remember.

105

'Didn't we? . . .' he started, and then hesitated, thinking.

'Do you make him, Cotton?'

'Not yet. Why? What's he done?'

'Says he killed a girl.'

'Yeah?'

'I was drunk when I said it.'

'Who was the girl?' Hawes asked, still staring at him.

'I don't have to answer you,' the man said.

'Got it!' Hawes said, and snapped his fingers. 'Your name's Roger Broome, we talked to you about a refrigerator that was stolen from the basement of a rooming house. This must've been three, four years ago. Am I right?'

The man remained silent.

'Is that your name?' Meyer said.

'Yes,' he said at last. 'That's my name.'

'What'd you say that beef was?' Meyer asked Hawes.

'Landlady over on Twelfth had a refrigerator swiped from her basement,' Hawes said. 'We questioned all her tenants. Mr Broome here was one of them.' He turned to Broome and said, 'I remember telling you I'd skied Mount Torrance. You live up there near Huddleston, don't you?'

'Yes, in Carey,' Broome said.

'Sure, I remember,' Hawes said.

'So now you're in trouble again,' Meyer said.

'I didn't steal her refrigerator!' Broome said.

'Then who did?'

'I don't know!'

'All right, don't get so excited.'

'I want a lawyer,' Broome said. 'I want to call my mother.'

'Just a little while ago, you said you *didn't* want a lawyer.'

'I want one now.'

'Why? You going to tell us what happened?'

'Nothing happened. I didn't steal her refrigerator.'

'But you *did* kill some girl, huh?'

'No. What's one thing got to do with the other?'

'I don't know, Mr Broome. Suppose *you* tell *us*.'

'I want to call my mother.'

106

'Why?'

'To tell her ... to let her know everything's all right. To ... to ... I want to call her.'

'I thought you wanted a lawyer?'

'Yes, I do.'

'Can you afford one, Mr Broome? Or shall we get one for you?'

'I don't know any lawyers in this city.'

'Shall we get one for you?'

'Yes. If you're going to trick me into saying things ...'

'We're not going to trick you into anything,' Meyer said. 'Cotton, call Legal Aid. We need a lawyer up here right away.'

'I asked for some coffee,' Broome said. 'Where's my coffee?'

'Breach!' Meyer yelled.

'Coming!' Breach yelled back.

It is difficult to determine why a man who has lived with guilt for such a long time will suddenly decide to tell everything. Go ask Theodore Reik. Perhaps, in the case of Roger Broome, it was merely the sudden appearance of Hawes that convinced him the jig was up. But then, how would that explain his getting up on a bar-room table and announcing to the world that he had killed a girl and got away with it?

Now, in the midnight stillness of the squad room, in the presence of two detectives, a police stenographer, and an appointed lawyer, Roger Broome told them everything, told them without any sense of relief, told them simply and directly and in a flat monotone about the girl he had met one winter, this must have been five years ago, no, it was only four, the month was February, a day or two before Valentine's Day, he could remember buying a card for his mother and also one for the landlady of the rooming house where he was staying, a woman named Mrs Dougherty. But that was after he had met the girl, after he had killed the girl.

The girl's name was Molly Nolan, she had come here to

107

the city from Sacramento, Canada, to look for a job. She was staying at a place called The Orquidea on Ainsley Avenue, he had met her in a bar, had a few drinks with her, and then had taken her back to his room at Mrs Dougherty's. She was a redheaded girl, not pretty, not at all pretty, but he had taken her to bed with him, and had told her she was beautiful, and then – he did not know why – he suddenly began hitting her, first in the eye, and then in the nose, making her bleed, and seeing that she was about to start screaming he had reached out quickly and grabbed her throat in his hands and squeezed her until she was dead.

He had carried her out of his room in the dead of night, down to the basement, where he had stuffed her into the old refrigerator after removing all the shelves. He had had to break both her legs to get her inside, he told them, and then he'd carried the refrigerator out to his truck and drove to a bridge someplace, he didn't remember the name of it but he could show them where it was, he had driven over that same bridge many times since and wondered each time if the refrigerator with the dead girl in it was still in the mud at the bottom of the river where he had dropped it that night so long ago.

He suddenly asked if the detective with the deaf and dumb wife still worked here, surprising them all, and then he began weeping and at last said, 'My mother'll kill me', and signed three copies of the typed confession.

It was nice to solve old cases.

The lady who had been stabbed, however, the lady named Margie Ryder was still with them.

EIGHT

At 10.0 AM on November 1st, Detective-Lieutenant Sam Grossman of the Police Laboratory called the 87th and asked to talk to Steve Carella. When Carella got on the line, Grossman told him a joke about a man who opened a pizza parlour across the street from the Vatican, and then got down to business.

'This electric razor,' he said.

'What electric razor?'

'The one we found in the bathroom of the Leyden apartment.'

'Right.'

'We dusted it for prints and discovered something very interesting.'

'What was that?'

'The prints belonged to the killer.'

'To Damascus?'

'Is that his name?'

'Well, let's say he's our prime suspect at the moment.'

'Why don't you pull him in?'

'Can't find him,' Carella said.

'Well, anyway, the fingerprints on the razor match the ones we found on the shotgun, so how about that?'

'I don't get it,' Carella said.

'Neither do I. Would you go shoot two people and then shave yourself with the dead man's razor?'

'No. Would you?'

'No. So why did *this* guy do it?'

'Maybe he needed a shave,' Carella suggested.

'Well, I guess I've heard stranger things,' Grossman said.

'So have I.'

'But why would he have taken such a risk? A shotgun

makes a hell of a lot of noise, Steve. Can you imagine a guy firing a shotgun *four* times, and then leisurely sauntering into the john to shave himself? With an electric razor, no less? It takes an *hour* to get a shave with one of those things.'

'Well, not *that* long.'

'However long,' Grossman said. 'You shoot two people, your first instinct is to get the hell out. You don't go take a shave with an electric razor.'

'Unless you know that the old lady across the hall is deaf and the only other apartment on the floor is empty.'

'You mean to tell me nobody else in the building heard those shots?'

'They heard them.'

'And?'

'The usual. Nobody called the police.'

'In any case, the killer must have known he'd made a lot of noise. He should have run.'

'But you're saying he didn't.'

'I'm saying he took a shave.'

'So what do you think?'

'I think you're dealing with a psycho,' Grossman said.

Gloria Leyden lived in a midtown apartment house on the edge of the River Dix. There was a doorman downstairs, and he stopped Carella and Kling in the lobby and then phoned upstairs to let Mrs Leyden know who was there. She promptly advised him to send them up, and they were whisked to the seventeenth floor by an elevator operator who kept whistling *I Don't Care Much* over and over again, off key.

The apartment overlooked the river, with wide sliding glass doors that opened on to a small terrace. The place was done in Danish modern, the walls white, the rugs beige. There was a clean, well-ordered look to everything. The four cats with whom Mrs Leyden shared the apartment seemed to have been chosen because they harmonized with the colour scheme. They moved suspiciously in and out of the living-room as the detectives questioned Mrs Leyden, stopping to sniff at Kling's cuff, and then at Carella's shoe, one after the other, as if they themselves were detectives checking and rechecking a doubtful piece of evidence. They made Kling nervous. He kept thinking they could smell Anne Gilroy on him.

'Mrs Leyden, we just wanted to ask you a few questions,' Carella said.

'Yes,' Mrs Leyden said, and nodded. It was eleven in the morning. She was wearing a belted housecoat, but she was clearly corseted beneath it. Her hair did not seem as violently lavender as it had that day in the mortuary. She sat perched on the edge of a chair covered in a nubby brown fabric, her back to the glass doors.

'To begin with, did you ever hear either your son or your daughter-in-law speaking of a man named Walter Damascus?'

'Walter *what*?'

'Damascus.'

'No. Never.'

'Walter *any*body?'

'No. None of their friends were named Walter.'

'Did you know many of their friends?'

'Some of them.'

'And your son never mentioned? . . .'

'No.'

'Nor your daughter-in-law?'

'I rarely spoke to my daughter-in-law,' Mrs Leyden said.

'Does that mean . . .'

'Never confidentially, anyway.'

'But you *were* on speaking terms?'

'Yes, we were on speaking terms.'

'Didn't you get along, Mrs Leyden?'

'We got along, I suppose. Are you asking me if I liked her?'

'*Did* you?'

'No.'

'I see.'

111

'I assure you, young man, that I do not know how to use a shotgun.'

'No one suggested . . .'

'My *son* was killed along with her, are you forgetting that?'

'Did you get along with *him*, Mrs Leyden?'

'Splendidly.'

'But not your daughter-in-law?'

'No. Not from the very beginning.'

'Which was when?'

'He brought her home from one of his trips. This must've been seven or eight years ago.'

'Where did she come from originally?'

'Alabama. He brings me home a Southern girl. You should have seen her. It was the summertime, she came into this very room wearing a tight yellow dress, straight out of Scarlett O'Hara. Some first impression.'

'What was her maiden name?'

'Rose Hilary Borden. They all use three names in the South, you know. She kept telling me about all her cousins, all of them with three names, Alice Mary Borden, and David Graham Borden and Horace Frank Borden, straight out of Scarlett O'Hara, you should have heard her. She was an only child herself, you know, but she had these thousands of cousins scattered all over the countryside, eating corn fritters and chitlings, I suppose. I told my son immediately that I didn't like her. Well, what can you do? He loved her, he said. Gave him a little poontang, I suppose, down South there on one of his lonely trips, men are all alike.'

Carella glanced at Kling. Neither of them said a word. Mrs Leyden nodded her head in agreement with her own philosophy, and then said, 'He was a very handsome boy, my son, he could have had any girl he wanted. Whenever he was on the road, the phone would ring every ten minutes, always another girl calling to ask when Andrew would be back. So he brings home Rose Hilary Borden in her tight yellow dress.'

'He was living here with you before they got married, is that it?' Kling asked.

'Yes, certainly. My husband passed away, poor soul, when Andrew was still a boy. You wouldn't expect a person to leave his widowed mother all alone, would you?'

'How old was he when he got married?' Carella asked.

'This was eight years ago, he was thirty-two.'

'And you said he met Rose down South, in Alabama?'

'Yes, Montgomery.'

'We understood his territory was in the West.'

'Not at that time. He was transferred three or four years ago, after they were married.'

'Tell me, Mrs Leyden, did you know your son would be coming home last weekend?'

'No.'

'He didn't call you?'

'No.'

'Did you speak to your daughter-in-law any time last weekend?'

'My daughter-in-law never called me when Andrew was away,' Mrs Leyden said. 'And *I* never called her, either.'

'We were just wondering if he'd told her he was coming. Apparently there'd been a change of plans . . .'

'I wouldn't know anything about that,' Mrs Leyden said. 'She didn't even tell me the time she was pregnant. I only found out after she lost the baby, and that was because Andrew mentioned it.'

'When was this?'

'In May.'

'She was pregnant and lost the baby?'

'Yes, in her second month.'

'Mrs Leyden, forgetting the name Walter Damascus for the moment, do you know of any of their friends who? . . .'

'No.'

'. . . might have harboured a grudge or . . .'

'No.'

'. . . for any reason whatever might have done something like this?'

'No,' Mrs Leyden said.

'And you've never heard of Walter Damascus?'

'No.'

So that was that. The cats sniffed around a bit longer, Mrs Leyden told the detectives again what a bitch her daughter-in-law was, and it was suddenly time for lunch.

It had been reasoned, perhaps incorrectly, that Walter Damascus might possibly return to his apartment to pick up the cheque he had left in his dresser drawer on the night of the Leyden murders. The theory behind such reasoning was simple: a man on the run needs money. So Detective Arthur Brown was assigned to a plant in Damascus' slovenly pad, and he sat alone there that Friday afternoon, a tall burly Negro who was darker than the darkness around him, wearing a blue cardigan sweater over a blue sports shirt, grey flannel slacks, his overcoat thrown over the back of a kitchen chair, his gun in his hand.

Brown did not like solitary plants, and he particularly disliked this one because the apartment stank and because there was nothing to see but the mess Damascus had left behind him. In an automobile stakeout, people kept coming and going, you watched the passing show, it was interesting. Even when you were planted in the back of a *store*, you could hear customers out front, you had a sense of life steadily moving, it was reassuring. Here, there was nothing but semi-darkness and silence. Damascus, whatever else he was, was most certainly a slob, and the smell in the apartment, combined with the darkness and the solitude, made Brown wish he had joined the Department of Sanitation instead. If he had, he would at this moment be riding a garbage truck that could not possibly stink as badly as this apartment did, and besides he would be outside in the crisp November sunshine. He debated raising the shades on the windows, decided against it, made himself comfortable in the wooden chair at the kitchen table, and was beginning to doze when he heard the key being inserted in the lock.

He was instantly awake and alert.

114

He rose and flattened himself against the kitchen wall as the door to the apartment opened. There was silence. The door closed again, cutting off the light from the corridor outside. There were footsteps into the room. They moved closer towards the kitchen doorway.

Brown hesitated only an instant longer, and then came around the door frame, gun extended, and curtly said, 'Hold it right there!'

He was looking into the startled face of a beautiful red-head.

Her name was Amanda Pope, and she asked the detective to please call her Mandy. She had come willingly to the station house, driving her own yellow Buick, Brown sitting beside her with his gun in his lap. She had chatted pleasantly with him on the short drive over, and now she sat pleasantly in the squad room surrounded by three cops who meant business, and she asked them to call her Mandy, and when advised of her rights said she had no need of a lawyer, she had done nothing wrong.

'What were you doing in that apartment?' Carella asked.

'I came to see Wally,' she said.

'Wally who?'

'Damascus.'

'Who gave you the key?'

'Wally did.'

'When?'

'Oh, months ago.'

She was a beautiful young lady, and she was well aware of her good looks, and she used them to expert advantage. charming the cops right out of their shoes. Her hair was a deep auburn, striking in combination with her fair complexion and large green eyes. Her nose was perfectly turned, tip-tilted and saucy. Her mouth was generous, she wore no lipstick, she sat in a straight-backed chair in a green woollen dress that swelled over her breasts and her hips. Her legs were crossed, splendid legs, her feet were encased in high-heeled green leather pumps that accented her slender ankles.

She looked up at the policemen and smiled dazzlingly, and each of them separately thought he would like to be questioning her alone in the Interrogation Room, instead of sharing her here in the squad room with his horny colleagues.

'What's your relationship with Damascus?' Kling asked.

'Oh, you know,' she said, and lowered her eyes demurely.

'Suppose you tell us,' Brown said.

'Well, we see a lot of each other,' Mandy said.

'How much?'

'A lot.'

'You living with him?'

'Not really.'

'What do you mean by that?'

They were finding it difficult to be stern with Amanda Pope because she was really so breathtakingly lovely and because feminine beauty is somehow associated with fragility and they did not want to run the risk of breaking or cracking or even chipping something as delicate as this. They felt enormously ashamed of the grubby surroundings to which they had introduced her, the grimy apple-green paint on the squad-room walls, the scarred desks, the dusty water cooler, the rusting metal grilles on all of the windows, the sombre filing cabinets, the detention cage fortunately empty at the moment. It was not often that beauty walked softly into these premises, and so they stood about her asking stern questions in their sternest manner, but they were beguiled, they were in fact almost hypnotized.

'Were you living with him or weren't you?' Carella asked.

'We had separate apartments,' Mandy said.

'Where's *your* apartment, Miss Pope?'

'Oh, please call me Mandy.'

Kling cleared his throat. 'Where's your apartment?' he repeated.

'Mandy,' she said, as though teaching a difficult word to a small child.

'Mandy,' Kling said, and then cleared his throat again.

'My apartment is on Randall and Fifth,' she said. Her

voice was as delicate as her beauty, she spoke clearly but softly, looking up at the detectives, the smile touching her mouth, behaving as though she were enjoying polite cocktail conversation in the presence of three charming and attentive men at an afternoon party.

'Now, Mandy,' Carella said, 'when's the last time you saw Damascus?'

'Last week,' she said.

'When last week?' Brown asked.

'Last Friday night.'

'Where'd you see him?'

'I picked him up at The Cozy Corners. That's a nightclub. He works there. He's a bouncer there.'

'What time'd you pick him up?'

'Closing time. Two o'clock.'

'Where'd you go from there?'

'To his apartment.'

'How long did you stay there?'

'In his apartment?'

'Yes.'

'An hour or so.'

'Doing what?'

'Well, you know,' Mandy said, and again lowered her eyes.

'And then what?' Kling asked.

'I drove him uptown.'

'Where uptown?'

'To South Engels.'

'Why?'

'It's where he wanted to go.'

'Did he say why?'

'Yes. He said there was a poker game he'd promised to go to.'

'So you drove him there.'

'Yes.'

'First you went to his apartment to make love, and then you drove him uptown to his poker game.'

'Yes.'

'What time was this?'

'Oh, I don't know exactly. It must have been some time between three and four in the morning.'

'And that was the last time you saw him?'

'Yes. When he got out of the car.'

'Have you seen him since?'

'No.'

'Talked to him?'

'No.'

'He hasn't called you?'

'No, he hasn't.'

'Have you called him?'

'He hasn't got a phone.' Mandy paused. 'Well I *did* call the club, but they said he hasn't been to work all week. So I thought I'd stop by the apartment this afternoon to see if anything was wrong.'

'Ever hear him mention some people named Leyden?'

'Layton? No.'

'Leyden. L-E-Y-D-E-N.'

'No, never.'

'Did he have anything with him when you left the apartment?'

'Like what?'

'Well, *you* tell *us*.'

'Yes, but I don't know what you mean.'

'Was he carrying a gun?'

'I don't think so. But I know he has a gun. A little pistol.'

'This would have been a big gun, Miss Pope . . .'

'Mandy.'

'. . . Mandy. You couldn't have missed it.'

'I still don't understand.'

'Miss Pope, was he carrying a shotgun?'

'A shotgun? No. Of course not. Why should he? . . .'

'Do you know what a shotgun looks like?'

'Well, no, but . . . well, yes, it's like a rifle, isn't it?'

'Somewhat.'

'No, I would have noticed something like that.'

'Was he carrying *any* sort of a large . . .'

'No.'

'... *anything* that could have been a shotgun wrapped up, or in a case ...'

'No, he wasn't carrying anything.'

'Mmm,' Carella said.

'Why would he take a gun to a poker game?' Mandy asked, and looked up at the cops.

'Maybe he wasn't going to a poker game, Miss Pope.'

'Mandy.'

'Maybe he was going uptown to kill some people.'

'Oh, no.'

'Some people named Rose and Andrew Leyden.'

'No,' Mandy said again.

'You're sure you haven't seen him since last Friday night?'

'Yes. And that's not like Wally, believe me. He'll usually call me three, four times a week.'

'But this week he hasn't called you at all?'

'Not once.'

'Did he mention anything about going out of town?'

'Where would he go?'

'*You* tell *us*.'

'No place. He has a job here. Why would he leave town?'

'If he killed some people, he might have decided it was best to leave town.'

'Well, I'm sure he didn't kill anyone.'

'Did you ever go out of town with him?'

'No.'

'Know if he has any relatives outside the city?'

'I don't know. He never mentioned any.'

'Miss Pope, if you ...'

'Mandy.'

'... hear from Damascus, I want you to call this squad room at once. I'm warning you now that he's suspected of having committed multiple homicide, and if you know of his whereabouts now ...'

'I *don't*.'

'... or learn of them at any time in the future, and

119

withhold this information from the police, you would then be considered an accessory.'

'Oh, I'm sure Wally hasn't killed anyone,' Mandy said.

'An accessory as described in Section 2 of the Penal Law, Miss Pope ... Mandy ... "is a person who, after the commission of a felony, harbours, conceals, or aids the offender, with intent that he may avoid or escape from arrest, trial, conviction or punishment, having knowledge or reasonable ground to believe that such offender is liable to arrest." Do you understand that?'

'Yes, I do. But Wally ...'

'We've just told you that if we find him we're going to arrest him, so you now have knowledge of that fact,' Brown said, and paused. 'Do you know where he is?'

'No, I'm sorry. I don't.'

'Will you call us if you hear from him?'

'Yes, of course I will. But you're really mistaken. Wally couldn't have killed anyone.'

'All right, Miss Pope, you're free to go now, Mandy,' Carella said.

'Show her out, somebody,' Kling said.

Brown showed her out.

NINE

EVERYBODY LIKES to spend Saturday in a different way.

Meyer and Hawes went to a poetry reading, Carella got hit on the head, and Bert Kling got beat up.

It was a nice Saturday.

The poetry reading was scheduled to start at 11 AM in the YMCA on Butler Street, but it did not actually get under way until 11.15, at which time a portly young man wearing muttonchop whiskers and a brown tweed suit stepped through the curtains and told the assembled crowd – some fifty people in all – that this was to be, as they all knew, a memorial service for Marguerite Ryder, who had been buried yesterday. The portly young man then went on to say that ten of Margie's closest friends and fellow poets had written elegies for her, and that they would be read by their authors this morning accompanied by the guitarist, Luis-Josafat Garzon. The portly young man then introduced Garzon, a sallow-faced gentleman wearing a dark-grey suit. Garzon solemnly sat on a black stool stage left, and the curtains opened, and the first poet stepped forward and began reading his tribute to the dead woman.

There was a curious mixture of mourning and celebration in that auditorium, an air of grief commingled with the excitement one might expect at a Broadway opening. The first poet read his work with dramatic fervour, as though hoping David Merrick was sitting in the audience with an offer to do a one-man show. In his poem, he compared Margie Ryder to a sparrow innocently striking an unexpected obstacle that had broken her body and snuffed out her life, 'to fly no more', he intoned, 'to fly no more, except in boundless dreams, eternal dreams'. He lowered his manuscript, his head, and his eyes. There was a brief silence, and Meyer fully expected everyone to begin applauding, thankful when they had the good grace not to. The second poet had titled his poem 'Voice', and in it he told of an incredibly lovely voice that had been stilled.

'Shout,' he shouted, *'scream against this indecency.*

'Raise your voice to raise the voice

'Robbed by the obscene steel of death!

'For oh, there was beauty here,

'There was depth and beauty enough

'To fill a garden,

'A forest,

'A world.

'Oh, Marge, we cry,

'We cry out!

'Our voices rise in tumultuous grievance!

'Hopefully you will hear and know, hear and know,

'Oh Marge.'

There was another silence. Hawes wanted to blow his nose, but was afraid to do so. Luis-Josafat Garzon played a brief, lugubrious guitar passage to cover the tardy entrance of the third poet, a tall gaunt young man wearing a beard and sunglasses. His poem, Hawes felt, was a trifle derivative, but the audience listened respectfully nonetheless, and there was even the sound of tears throughout the reading.

'It was only a week or so ago,

'As I sat sipping my cider,

'That a woman was killed whom you may know,

'By the name of Marguerite Ryder.

'And this woman she lived with no other thought

'Than to give to the humans beside her.'

Hawes looked at Meyer, and Meyer looked at Hawes, and the gaunt, bearded, sunglassed poet began reading the second stanza.

'She was a child, yes only a child,

'In a tenement garden of dreams,

'And the love that she gave, was a love more than love,

'But it ended in futile screams.

122

'*Someone tore her apart, someone stepped on her heart,*
'*Someone viciously opened her seams.*'

The reading continued in a similar vein for the remainder of the morning. Unlike the assorted poets who read their wares, the audience seemed composed of people who could hardly be classed as hippies. A spot check of the crowd turned up neighbourhood faces familiar to Hawes and Meyer alike; merchants, housewives, professional men, even a patrolman from their own precinct, sitting attentively in his off-duty clothes. The idea, of course, was not to glom the audience, but rather to take a bead on 'ten of Margie's closest friends', any of whom might have done the dear girl in.

Discounting the mystery man who had met Margie in Perry's Bar & Grille on DeBeck Avenue, and who had later returned in desperate need of her name, discounting him as a prime suspect because there were too many ifs involved (*if* he had finally remembered her name, and *if* he had gone to her apartment, and *if* she had let him in at that hour of the morning), there remained the likelihood that the person who had stabbed Margie was indeed one of her good friends, someone who *could* have been with her in her apartment at four or later in the morning. So Meyer and Hawes sat through two hours and ten minutes of bad poetry (including some lines attributed to Marguerite Ryder herself) while pretending they were at a police line-up instead, an entertainment now defunct but not missed in the slightest by either of the men.

The parade of poets was colourful but hardly instructive. Meyer and Hawes went backstage after the reading to talk to the ten budding versifiers, as well as to the guitarist Garzon. They learned to their surprise that there had been a party at Garzon's house on the night Margie was murdered, with 'Mos' of the kids' (as Garzon put it) having been in attendance.

'Was Margie Ryder there?' Hawes asked.

'Oh, yes,' Garzon said.

'What time did she leave?'

'She ony stay a shor' while.'

'How long?'

'She arrive abou' ten o'clock, and she leave it mus' have been close to mi'night.'

'Alone?'

'*Perdone?*'

'Did she leave the party alone?'

'Ah, *sí, sí. Solo.* Alone.'

'Was she with anyone in particular while she was there?'

'No, she drift aroun', *comprende*? It wass like a big party, you know? So she stop here, she stop there, she drink, she laugh, she wass *muy* sociable, Margie, you know? Everybody like her.'

Which did not explain why anybody would want to kill her.

Meyer and Hawes thanked everybody and went out into the street to breathe some fresh November prose.

Steve Carella was supposed to take down the screens, but he decided to visit the Leyden apartment instead, which is how he happened to get hit on the head. Of course, he might have got hit on the head while taking down the screens too, but in police work there is a clear line between possibility and probability, and chances were a good sixty-to-one that he would not have been nursing a bump on his noggin that night if he had taken care of his household duties that afternoon, instead of running into the city to snoop around an empty apartment.

The reason he went back to the apartment was not, as Teddy had surmised, to get out of taking down the screens. (True, he did not enjoy taking down screens, but neither did he enjoy putting them up, and he enjoyed getting hit on the head perhaps even less than either.) He had discovered through years of police work that very often you can't see the forest for the trees, which is a fresh and imaginative way of saying that sometimes you have to step back for a long view, or closer for a tight view, in order to regain your perspective on a case.

In Carella's thinking, a murder invariably served as the impetus that set in action a proscribed police routine. Often, in slogging through reports typed in triplicate, in deciphering the medical gobbledegook on an autopsy return, in tailing a suspect or interrogating a witness, in poring over questioned documents or ballistics data, it was completely possible to forget *why* you were doing all these things, forget that it was indeed a *corpse* that had prompted this machinery into motion. When that happened, he found it advisable to return to the scene, and imagine for himself the details of what *might* have happened during the actual commission of the crime.

Also, he hated taking down screens.

The elevator sped him to the third floor. It was a self-service elevator, and the killer could have used it with immunity at any hour of the day or night – but *had* he? Would he have risked being seen by, say, a pair of tenants returning home from a late party? Or would he have more realistically used the stairway which opened directly on to the apartment's service entrance? After all, the kitchen door had been found open by Novello, the milkman. Wasn't it likely that the killer had entered and left by the same door? Standing on the corridor, Carella looked at the closed front door to Mrs Leibowitz's apartment, heard behind it the singing of her coloured maid, and then walked down the hall to the Pimm apartment. He listened at the door. The apartment within was still.

He went back up the hallway again to the Leyden apartment, decided to enter instead by the service entrance, and walked to the small *cul de sac* at the end of the corridor. The garbage cans for all three apartments were stacked on the small landing there. The back doors to the Leibowitz and Pimm apartments were on one side of the landing, the back door to the Leyden apartment opposite them. Without trying to figure out what was obviously a complicated architectural scheme, Carella reached into his side pocket for the key he had signed out downtown at the Office of the Clerk yesterday (Premeditation, Teddy would claim, you knew you weren't going to take down those screens today) and approached the Leydens' kitchen door. He had a little trouble turning the key in the lock (Should be using my goddamn skeleton, he thought) but finally managed to twist it and open the door. He had a bit more trouble extricating the key, yanked it loose at last, put it back into his side pocket, and closed the door behind him.

The apartment was silent.

This is where the killer must have stood, he thought. He must have entered through this door, and hesitated for a moment in the kitchen, trying to determine where his victims were. Rose Leyden had doubtless heard something and come into the living-room to investigate, and that was when he'd fired the two shots that had taken off her face.

Carella moved into the living-room.

The rug was still stained, the blood having dried to a muddy brown colour. He looked down at the huge smear where Rose Leyden's head had rested, and then glanced towards the bedroom. Andrew Leyden had probably been asleep, exhausted after his long trip home, shocked into wakefulness by the two shots that had killed his wife. He had most likely jumped out of bed, perhaps yelling his wife's name (Was that the shouting one of the tenants had reported hearing?) and started for the living-room only to be met by the killer in the bedroom doorway.

Carella nodded, and walked across the room.

The killer probably stopped right here, he thought, firing into Leyden's face, you have to hate somebody a hell of a lot to fire a shotgun at point-blank range into his face. *Twice.* Carella took a step into the bedroom. He saw that the top drawer of the dresser was open, and he recalled instantly that it had not been open on the morning after the murders, and he wondered whether the lab boys had left it that way, and he was starting towards the dresser to investigate when somebody came from behind the door and hit him on the head.

He thought as he fell towards the bedroom floor that

you can get stupid if people hit you on the head often enough and then, stupidly, he lost consciousness.

It is easy to solve murder cases if you are alert.

It is also easy to get beat up if you are not careful. Bert Kling was not too terribly alert that afternoon, and so he did not come even close to solving the Leyden case. Being careless, he got beat up

He got beat up by a woman.

Anne Gilroy marched up the front steps of the station house at ten minutes to three, wearing a blue-and-red striped mini, her long blonde hair caught at the back of her neck with a red ribbon. Her shoes were blue, they flashed with November sunshine as she mounted the steps and walked past the green globes flanking the stoop. She walked directly to where Sergeant Dave Murchison sat behind the high muster desk, beamed a radiant smile at him, batted her blue eyes in a semaphore that even desk sergeants understood, and sweetly said, 'Is Detective Kling in?'

'He is,' Murchison said.

'May I see him, please?'

'Who shall I say is here, whom?' Murchison said.

'Miss Anne Gilroy,' she said and wheeled away from the desk to study first the wanted posters on the bulletin board, and then the clock on the wall. She sat at last on the wooden bench opposite the muster desk, took out a cigarette from her blue bag, glanced inquiringly at Murchison before lighting it (He nodded permission) and then, to his distraction, crossed her legs and sat calmly smoking while he tried to reach Kling, who was at that moment in the lieutenant's office.

'Tied up right now,' Murchison said. 'Would you mind waiting a moment?'

'Thank you,' Anne Gilroy said, and jiggled her foot. Murchison looked at her legs, wondering what the world was coming to, and wondering whether he should give permission to his twelve-year-old daughter, prepubescent and emerging, to wear such short skirts when she entered her teens, see clear up the whole leg, he thought, and then mopped his brow and plugged into the switchboard as a light flashed. He held a brief conversation, pulled out the cord, looked again to where Anne Gilroy sat with crossed legs and smoke-wreathed blonde hair, and said, 'He'll be right down, miss'.

'Oh, can't I go up?'

'He said he'd be down.'

'I was hoping to see a squad room.'

'Well,' Murchison said, and tilted his head to one side, and thought, what the hell do you hope to see up there except a few bulls working their asses off? The switchboard blinked into life again. He plugged in and took a call from an irate patrolman on Third who said he had phoned in for a meat wagon half an hour ago and there was a lady bleeding on the goddamn sidewalk, when was it gonna *get* there? Murchison told him to calm down, and the patrolman told Murchison he had never seen so much blood in his life and the lady was gonna die, and the crowd was getting mean. Murchison said he'd call the hospital again, and then yanked out the cord, and gave himself an outside line.

He was dialling the hospital when Kling came down the iron-runged steps leading from the second floor. Kling looked surprised, even though Murchison had told him who was here. Maybe it was the short skirt that did it. Murchison watched as Kling walked to the bench ('Hello, this is Sergeant Murchison over at the 87th Precinct,' he said into the phone, 'where the hell's that ambulance?') extended his hand to Anne Gilroy and then sat on the bench beside her. Murchison could not hear them from across the room. ('Well, I got a patrolman screaming at me, and a crowd about to get unmanageable, and a lady about to bleed to death right on the sidewalk there, so how about it?') Kling now seemed more embarrassed than surprised, he kept nodding his head at Anne Gilroy as she smiled and batted her blue eyes, talking incessantly, her face very close to his as though she were whispering all the secrets of

128

the universe to him. ('Yeah, well how about breaking up the goddamn pinochle game and getting somebody over there?' Murchison shouted into the phone.) Kling nodded again, rose from the bench and walked towards the muster desk. ('If I get another call from that patrolman, I'm going straight to the Mayor's office, you got that?' Murchison yelled, and angrily pulled the cord from the switchboard.)

'I'm going out for some coffee,' Kling said.

'Okay,' Murchison said. 'When will you be back?'

'Half an hour or so.'

'Right,' Murchison said, and watched as Kling went back to the bench. Anne Gilroy stood up, looped her arm through Kling's, smiled over her shoulder at Murchison, and clickety-clacked on her high heels across the muster-room floor, tight little ass twitching busily, long blonde hair bouncing on her back. The switchboard was glowing again. Murchison plugged in to find the same patrolman, nearly hysterical this time because the lady had passed away a minute ago, and her brother was screaming to the crowd that this was police negligence, and the patrolman wanted to know what to do. Murchison said whatever he did, he shouldn't draw his revolver unless it got really threatening, and the patrolman told him it looked really threatening right *now*, with the crowd beginning to yell and all, and maybe he ought to send some reinforcements over. Murchison said he'd see what he could do and that was when the scream came from the front steps outside the precinct.

Murchison was a desk cop, and he wasn't used to re-acting too quickly, but there was something urgent about this scream, and he put two and two together immediately and realized that the person screaming must be the girl named Anne Gilroy who had sashayed out of here just a minute ago on the arm of Bert Kling. He came around the muster desk with all the swiftness of a corpulent man past fifty, reaching for his holstered revolver as he puffed to-wards the main doors, though he couldn't understand what could possibly be happening on the front steps of a police station, especially to a girl who was in the company of a detective.

What was happening – and this surprised Murchison no end because he expected to find a couple of hoods maybe threatening the girl or something – what was happening was that *another* blonde girl was hitting Kling on the head with a dispatch case. It took a moment for Murchison to recognize the other blonde girl as Cindy Forrest, whom he had seen around enough times to know that she was Kling's girl, but he had never seen her with such a terrible look on her face. The only time he had ever seen a woman with such a look on her face was the time his Aunt Moira had caught his Uncle John screwing the lady upstairs on the front-room sofa of her apartment. Aunt Moira had gone up to get a recipe for glazed oranges and had got instead her glassy-eyed husband humping the bejabbers out of the woman who until then had been her very good friend. Aunt Moira had chased Uncle John into the hallway and down the steps with his pants barely buttoned, hitting him on the head with a broom she grabbed on the third-floor landing, chasing Uncle John clear into the streets where Murchison and some of his boyhood friends were playing Knuckles near Ben the Kosher Delicatessen. The look on Aunt Moira's face had been something terrible and fiery to see, all right, and the same look was on Cindy Forrest's young and pretty face this very moment as she continued to clobber Kling with the brown leather dispatch case. The blonde girl, Anne Gilroy, kept screaming for her to stop, but there was no stopping a lady when she got the Aunt Moira look. Kling, big detective that he was, was trying to cover his face and the top of his head with both hands while Cindy did her demolition work. The girl Anne Gilroy kept screaming as Murchison rushed down the steps yelling, 'All right, break it up', sounding exactly like a cop. The only thing Cindy seemed intent on breaking up, however, was Kling's head, so Murchison stepped between them, gingerly avoiding the flailing dispatch case, and then shoved Kling down the steps and out of range, and shouted at Cindy, 'You're striking a police officer, miss', which she undoubtedly knew, and the girl Anne Gilroy screamed once again, and then there was silence.

'You rotten son of a bitch,' Cindy said to Kling.

'It's all right, Dave,' Kling said from the bottom of the steps. 'I can handle it.'

'Oh, you certainly can handle it, you bastard,' Cindy said.

'Are you all right?' Anne Gilroy asked.

'I'm fine, Anne,' Kling answered.

'Oh, *Anne* is it?' Cindy shouted, and swung the dispatch case at her. Murchison stepped into the line of fire, deflected the case with the back of his arm, and then yanked Cindy away from the girl and shouted, 'Now goddamn you, Cindy, do you want to wind up in the cooler?'

By this time a crowd of patrolmen had gathered in the muster room, embarrassing Kling, who liked to maintain a sort of detective-superiority over the rank and file. The patrolmen were enormously entertained by the spectacle of Sergeant Murchison trying to keep apart two very dishy blondes, one of whom happened to be Kling's girl, while Kling stood by looking abashed.

'All right, break it up,' Kling said to them, also sounding like a cop. The other cops thought this was amusing, but none of them laughed. Neither did any of them break it up. Instead, they crowded into the doorway, ogled the girl in the red-and-blue mini, ogled Cindy too (even though she was more sedately dressed in a blue shift), and then glanced first to Kling and then to Murchison to see who would make the next move.

Neither of them did.

Instead, Cindy turned on her heel, tilted her nose up, and marched down the steps and past Kling.

'Cindy, wait, let me explain!' Kling cried, obviously thinking he was in an old Doris Day movie, and immediately ran up the street after her.

'I want to press charges,' Anne Gilroy said to Murchison.

'Oh, go home, miss,' Murchison said, and then went up the steps and shoved past the patrolmen in the doorway and

131

went back to the switchboard, where the most he'd have to contend with was something like a lady bleeding to death on the sidewalk.

Carella wondered why everybody always seemed to swim up out of unconsciousness. He himself was suddenly and completely conscious, no swimming up, no dizzying ascending spiral, none of that crap, he merely opened his eyes, and knew exactly where he was, and got to his feet and felt the very large bump at the back of his head, felt it first as a radiating nucleus of pain in his skull, then actually touched it with his fingertips, causing it to hurt even more. There was no blood, thank God for that, his attacker had spared him the indignity of a cracked skull. Belatedly, he looked behind the door just to make sure another little surprise wasn't being planned, and then drew his revolver and went through each room of the apartment because it's always good to lock the barn door after the horse has gone. Satisfied that he was alone, he went back to the bedroom.

The top dresser drawer was closed.

It had been open when he'd come into the apartment, so it was reasonable to assume he'd surprised an intruder in the act of ransacking it. He went to it now and began doing a little ranksacking himself. The drawer was divided into clearly masculine and feminine halves. On Rose Leyden's side of the drawer there were nylon stockings, panties, garter belts, bras and handkerchiefs, as well as a small circular tin box once containing throat lozenges but now holding stray ear-rings, bobby pins, and buttons. On Andrew Leyden's side there were socks (blue solids, black solids, and grey solids), handkerchiefs, undershorts, a lone athletic supporter and, at the very rear of the drawer, a mint-condition Kennedy half-dollar. Carella closed the drawer and then went through the rest of the dresser. Rose Leyden's side contained folded sweaters, blouses, slips, scarves, and nightgowns. Andrew Leyden's side contained ironed dress shirts and sports shirts, and folded sweaters. Carella closed the last drawer and walked to the closet.

The same system seemed to apply here as did in the dresser. The single clothes bar was again divided, with Rose Leyden's dresses, slacks, and suits occupying perhaps two-thirds of the space, and Andrew Leyden's suits, trousers and sports jackets filling the remaining third. His ties were on a tie bar nailed to the inside of the door. A shoe rack ran the length of the closet. Rose's pumps and slippers rested on it beneath her hanging clothes; Andrew's were on the rack below *his* clothes. Everything very neat, everything His and Hers.

So what had the intruder wanted in the top dresser drawer?

And had the intruder been Walter Damascus?

Carella's head began to hurt a little more.

Kling used his own key on the door, and then twisted the knob, and shoved the door inward, but Cindy had taken the precaution of fastening the safety chain, and the door abruptly jarred to a stop, open some two and a half inches, but refusing to budge farther.

'Cindy,' he shouted, 'take off this chain! I want to talk to you.'

'I don't want to talk to you!' she shouted back.

'Take off this chain, or I'll break the door off the hinges!'

'Go break you bimbo's door, why don't you?'

'She's not a bimbo!'

'Don't defend her, you louse!' Cindy shouted.

'Cindy, I'm warning you, I'll kick this door in!'

'You do, and I'll call the police!'

'I *am* the police.'

'Go police your bimbo, louse.'

'Okay, honey, I warned you.'

'You'd better have a search warrant,' she shouted, 'or I'll sue you *and* the city *and* the . . .'

Kling kicked in the door efficiently and effortlessly. Cindy stood facing him with her fists clenched.

'Don't come in here,' she said. 'You're not wanted here.

133

You're not wanted here ever again. Go home. Go away. Go to hell.'

'I want to talk to you.'

'I don't want to talk to you ever again as long as I live, that's final.'

'What are you so sore about?'

'I don't like liars and cheats and rotten miserable liars. Now get out of here, Bert, I mean it.'

'Who's a liar?'

'*You* are.'

'How am I . . .'

'You said you loved me.'

'I *do* love you.'

'Ha!'

'That girl . . .'

'That *slut* . . .'

'She's not a slut.'

'That's right, she's a sweet Irish virgin. Go hold her hand a little, why don't you? Get out of here, Bert, before I hit you again.'

'Listen, there's nothing . . .'

'That's right, there's nothing, there's absolutely nothing between us ever again, get out of here.'

'Lower your voice, you'll have the whole damn building in here.'

'All snuggly-cosy, arm-in-arm, batting her eyes . . .'

'She had information . . .'

'Oh, I'll just *bet* she has information.'

'. . . about the Leyden case She came to the squad room . . .'

'I'll just *bet* she has information,' Cindy repeated, a bit hysterically, Kling thought. 'I'll bet she has information even *Cleopatra* never dreamt of. Why don't you get out of here and leave me alone, okay? Just get out of here, okay? Go get all that hot information, okay?'

'Cindy . . .'

'I thought we were in love . . .'

'We *are*.'

134

'I thought we . . .'

'We *are*, dammit!'

'I thought we were going to get married one day and have kids and live in the country . . .'

'Cindy . . .'

'So a cheap little floozie flashes a smile and . . .'

'Cindy, she's a nice girl who . . .'

'Don't you *dare*!' Cindy shouted. 'If you're here to *defend* that little tramp . . .'

'I'm *not* here to defend her!'

'Then why *are* you here?'

'To tell you I love you.'

'Ha!'

'I love you,' Kling said.

'Yeah.'

'I do.'

'Yeah.'

'I love you.'

'Then why . . .'

'We were going out for a cup of coffee, that's all.'

'Sure.'

'There's nobody in the whole world I want but you,' Kling said.

Cindy did not answer.

'I mean it.'

She was still silent.

'I love you, honey,' he said. 'Now come on.' He waited. She was standing with her head bent, watching the floor. He did not dare approach her. 'Come on,' he said.

'I wanted to kill you,' Cindy said softly. 'When I saw you together, I wanted to kill you.' She began weeping gently, still staring at the floor, not raising her eyes to his. He went to her at last and took her in his arms, and held her head cradled against his shoulder, his fingers lightly stroking her hair, her tears wetting his jacket and his shirt.

'I love you so much,' she said, 'that I wanted to kill you.'

TEN

ON SUNDAY afternoon, Mr and Mrs George Pimm returned from their vacation in Puerto Rico and were promptly visited by the police.

They were in the midst of unpacking when Carella and Kling arrived. It was difficult to keep them to the point. This had been their first trip to the Caribbean, and they were naturally anxious to tell someone – anyone – all about it. Unfortunately, the detectives were the first people they'd seen since their return.

'A wonderful island,' Pimm said. 'Have you ever been there?'

'No,' Carella said.

'No,' Kling said.

'Well, what's your sight-unseen impression of it, would you tell me that?' Pimm said. He was a slender man with bright blue eyes and sandy-coloured hair. He had acquired a deep tan on the island, and he unpacked now with all the sureness and vigour of a person who feels and looks healthy. His wife, Jeanine, was a petite brunette who kept carrying things to the dresser and the closet and the bathroom as Pimm took them from the suitcases. She was already beginning to peel, especially on the nose. She kept smiling as Pimm discussed the island. 'If you judge from this city,' Pimm said, 'you expect Puerto Ricans to be misfits, don't you? Drug addicts, and street fighters and prostitutes, and what not, excuse me, honey,' he said to his wife.

'That's all right, George,' Jeanine said, smiling.

'But believe me, they are the sweetest, gentlest people in the world,' Pimm said. 'Well, look, we came out of El Convento, that's a hotel down there in the heart of Old San Juan, we came out of there one night after the dinner and

136

floor show – wonderful floor show, by the way – and oh, it must've been after midnight, wasn't it after midnight, honey?'

'Oh, yes, easily after midnight,' Jeanine said.

'Now, can you imagine walking in the Puerto Rican section of this city after midnight? Along the Spanish stretch of Culver Avenue, say? After midnight? No reflection on the work you fellows do,' Pimm said, 'but that'd be taking your life in your hands, am I right?'

'Well, all slum areas are pretty much alike,' Carella said. 'I wouldn't want to walk along *Ainsley* after midnight, either.'

'George is even afraid of walking downtown on Hall Avenue,' Jeanine said, and smiled.

'That's not true,' Pimm said. 'Hall Avenue is perfectly safe. Isn't it perfectly safe?' he asked Carella.

'Well, there've been muggings in *good* neighbourhoods too. But I guess Hall Avenue is fairly safe.'

'Anyway, that's not my point,' Pimm said. 'My point is, there we were in the heart of Old San Juan, walking the streets after midnight, Jeanine all dolled up, both of us *surrounded* by Puerto Ricans, the only tourists walking around down there so late at night, but were we afraid anything would happn? Absolutely not! We felt perfectly safe, we felt those people meant us no harm, were in fact glad to have us there and anxious to make us welcome. Now, why should that be?'

'Why should *what* be?'

'Why should they come to this city and start throwing garbage out the windows, and start living like pigs, and taking dope, and selling their sisters and causing trouble everyplace? Why should that be?'

'Maybe they're better hosts than *we* are,' Carella said.

'Huh?'

'Maybe if we made *them* feel safe, things would be a little different.'

'Well, anyway,' Pimm said dubiously, 'it's a beautiful island.'

'Tell them about *El Junque*,' Jeanine suggested.

'Oh, yeah, *El Junque*, that's the Rain Forest. You go into this enormous forest . . .'

'A jungle, really,' Jeanine said.

'Right, a jungle,' Pimm said, '*this is the forest primeval*,' he quoted, 'and . . .'

'Mr Pimm,' Carella said, 'I know you're anxious to get on with your unpacking, and this is probably an inconvenient time . . .'

'No, no, not at all,' Pimm said, 'we can unpack while we talk, can't we, Jeanine?'

'Oh, sure, there isn't much more to do anyway.'

'Well, we don't want to take up too much of your time,' Carella said. 'We were wondering if you'd heard anything about the Leyden murders while you were south.'

'Yes, it was in the newspapers. Terrible thing,' Pimm said.

'Terrible,' Jeanine repeated.

'Did you know them well?'

'As well as you get to know anybody in an apartment house,' Pimm said. 'You know the old cliché. People can live next door to each other for years without ever knowing each other's names.'

'Yes, but you *did* know the Leydens?'

'Never been in there, if that's what you mean,' Pimm said.

'Well, George, we've only lived in the building a year.'

'Little more than a year,' Pimm said.

'And you've never been inside the Leyden apartment?'

'No, never.'

'Well, I was in there once,' Jeanine said.

'When was that?'

'She was sick one morning. I met her downstairs doing the laundry. In the basement. She looked awfully pale, I thought she might faint or something. So I came upstairs with her into the apartment. She got sick in the bathroom.'

'When was this, Mrs Pimm?'

'In April, I think it was. Yes, it was a little after the beginning of April.'

'When you say she got "sick" in the bathroom, do you mean? . . .'

'Yes, she threw up.'

'She was pregnant, wasn't she?' Pimm asked. 'Isn't that what Mrs Leibowitz said?'

'Yes, later on we found out she was pregnant. Mrs Leibowitz told us she lost the baby. That's our next-door neighbour.'

'Yes, we've met her,' Kling said.

'A nice lady,' Pimm said.

'She's deaf,' Jeanine said.

'Well, a little hard of hearing,' Pimm said.

'But aside from that one time in the apartment . . .'

'That's right,' Jeanine said.

'. . . you were never in there, never really friendly?'

'That's right.'

'Nor did she visit you.'

'Well, they kept to themselves, you know. He was on the road a lot, he's a travelling salesman, you know . . .'

'Yes.'

'. . . sells heavy machinery, I think.'

'Tractors,' Jeanine said.

'That's right.'

'Yes.'

'So he was hardly ever around, you know, gone for months at a time.'

'I'd see her down in the basement every now and then,' Jeanine said. 'Or in the elevator. You know. Like that.'

'She was a nice girl,' Pimm said. 'Seemed to be, anyway.'

'Yes,' Jeanine said.

'Introduced me to her brother once,' Pimm said. 'Nice fellow, too. Met them coming out of the apartment one day.'

'Her *brother*?' Carella said. He had just remembered with a chilling suddenness that Gloria Leyden had described her daughter-in-law as an only child. *She was an only child herself, you know, but she had these thousands of cousins scattered all over the countryside.*

'That's right, her brother,' Pimm said.

139

'What'd he look like?'

'Tall fellow, very good-looking. Blue eyes, dark hair. Nice fellow.'

'What was his name? Did she say?'

'Harry, I think.'

'No,' Jeanine said.

'Wasn't it Harry?' Pimm asked.

'Wally,' Jeanine said. 'It was Wally.'

So now the closet door was open and as usual there was a skeleton hanging in it. The skeleton was a familiar one, it bored Carella and Kling to tears. Oh, how they hoped for an original slaying once in a while, a well-conceived murder instead of these sloppy run-of-the-mill crimes of passion that were constantly being dumped into their laps. Oh, how they longed for a killer who would knock off somebody with a rare untraceable poison, Oh, how they wished they might find a body in a locked windowless room, Oh, how they wanted somebody to scheme and plot for months on end and then commit the perfect homicide which everyone would think was suicide or something. Instead, what did they get? They got Andrew Leyden, cuckold of the month, working his little heart out in California and environs while Rosie dallied with her lover. They got Walter Damascus, womanizer supreme, with his Mandy downtown and his Rosie uptown, who for whatever twisted reasons of his own decided he would knock off both his uptown mistress and her husband. Walter Damascus, who had committed murder crudely and brutally and then oh so cleverly rigged the second murder to look like suicide – a clumsy ruse that would be detected the moment any apprentice cop found the ejected shotgun shell. That was what they got. They got a crazy bastard who made love to Mandy downtown in his pigsty apartment, asked her to drive him uptown to his 'poker game', blasted Rosie and Andy, and then went into the john to shave with the dead man's razor.

They never got the interesting cases.

Meyer and Hawes got all the interesting ones.

140

The interesting thing about the Margie Ryder case was that there seemed to be no motive. The other interesting thing was that it was very neat for a stabbing. When somebody starts stabbing another person, there's a certain *je ne sais quoi* that takes over, a rhythm that's established, a compulsive need to plunge the blade again and again, so it shouldn't be a total loss. It is not uncommon in stabbings to find a corpse with anywhere from a dozen to a hundred wounds, that's the thing about stabbings.

Margie Ryder was stabbed only once.

Once is enough, you may say, because after all if you've seen one kitchen knife being plunged into your chest, you've seen them all. But it was this very *lack* of multiple wounds that ran contrary to what the police had come to expect in all the dreary little knifings they encountered every day of the week.

Nothing had been stolen from the Ryder apartment, nor had the woman been molested. Discounting burglary then, and discounting rape, the bartender Jim Martin seemed to have a point when he suggested that the killer *had* to be somebody Margie knew. Well, most of the people she'd known had been at a party thrown by the guitarist Luis-Josafat Garzon, and she had left that party alone, and had then proceeded to Perry's Bar & Grille on DeBeck Avenue where, according to Martin's volunteered information, she had been in conversation half the night with a stranger. That stranger had returned later to ask her name, and then might (oh boy, what a big *might*) have remembered it, and gone to her apartment, and been let in by Maggie, and had stabbed her. Why had he forgotten her name to begin with? And what caused him to remember it again? And why had she let him in at four in the morning? Interesting, right? Meyer and Hawes got all the interesting ones.

But the most interesting thing about it was the lack of motivation. It almost seemed – and this was very puzzling – it almost seemed as if the man, the stranger become acquaintance, had gone there specifically to kill her. There were no signs of a struggle, there was no torn clothing or toppled furniture, no indication that there had been a violent argument, nothing even in the stabbing itself to indicate the actions of a man gone berserk, a man unable to control the terrible destructive power of a plunging blade. Everything was neat and simple, Margie in basic black and pearls, the knife sticking out of her chest, the single stab wound.

Neat.

Simple.

Interesting.

It stank.

On Monday afternoon, everything almost cracked wide open.

The bank teller called at 4 PM. Steve Carella took the call. The teller explained that he had first called Police Headquarters to ask who was handling the Leyden case he'd been reading so much about in the newspapers. Headquarters had informed him that Detectives Carella and Kling of the 87th Precinct were handling the case, and then had belatedly asked the teller what his name was, and he had said Derek Heller, and then had given his address and telephone number at their request, and had asked whether he might talk directly to either of the two detectives handling the case. The man at Headquarters had grunted and grumbled and then reluctantly told Heller to call Frederick 7–8024, which he was doing now.

'Are you Detective Carella?' he asked.

'I'm Detective Carella.'

'How do you do? Mr Carella, I think I have some information that might help you.'

'Regarding the Leyden case?'

'Yes, sir, regarding that case,' Heller said. 'I've read an awful lot about it in the newspapers, which is why I'm calling.'

'Yes, Mr Heller?'

'I'm the head teller at Commerce of America. We've got seven branches in the city, including one uptown on Ainsley Avenue, which is in your precinct.'

'Yes, Mr Heller?'

'I work at the branch on Aley and Harris, all the way donwtown here.'

'Yes, Mr Heller?'

'I'll have to give you this in sequence because it only came to my attention through a coincidental series of events.'

'Take your time, Mr Heller.'

'Well, we close at three o'clock, as you know, and one of our tellers was having some difficulty proving his drawer. He was a dollar and thirty cents short, nothing to get terribly upset about, but he's a new teller, and well, these things happen. In any event, he asked my assistance, and we began going through the drawer – the cash, the cheques, all of it. That was how I happened to notice this one cheque. Mind you, I wasn't looking for it. I was looking for that dollar-thirty discrepancy.'

'Yes, go on, Mr Heller.'

'The cheque I'm talking about was made out to cash.'

'For how much?'

'Two hundred dollars, and drawn on our bank. That is to say, the checking account is one of ours.'

'Yes, Mr Heller?'

'It is, in fact, one of our regular checking accounts, as opposed to our special checking accounts. With the special accounts, as you may know, there is a small charge for each cheque written. Our *regular* accounts, on the other hand ...'

'Well, what about this *particular* cheque, Mr Heller?'

'It was drawn to the account of Rose and Andrew Leyden of 561 South Engels Street in Isola.'

'Well, why do you find that unusual, Mr Heller?'

'I don't. The cheque is dated October sixteenth, and I know that Mr Leyden wasn't killed until October twenty-eighth, so there's nothing unusual about it coming in to be cashed at this time. I'm talking about the endorsement. *That's* what's unusual.'

'What do you mean?'

'The man who endorsed the cheque forged Andrew Leyden's signature.'

*　　　*　　　*

143

Edward Graham, the teller at the Aley and Harris Streets branch of Commerce of America, was a frightened young man who was afraid he would lose his job. Derek Heller kept assuring him he had done nothing wrong, but the presence of two detectives fairly sent him crawling into the vault, and they and Heller had a difficult job trying to calm him down. Heller was a thin, distinguished-looking man of about thirty-eight, wearing a grey suit and black tie. There was an inkstain on the collar of his otherwise immaculate white shirt. He spoke softly and earnestly to Graham, who finally gained control of himself, at least enough to answer the questions Carella and Kling put to him.

'What time did this man come in, Mr Graham, would you remember that?'

'Yes, it was just before noon.'

'Would you remember what he looked like?'

'He was a tall man, good-looking, well-dressed.'

'What colour hair did he have?'

'Dark.'

'And his eyes?'

'I don't remember.'

'What happened, can you tell us exactly?'

'He gave me the cheque, and asked for the money in tens.'

'Did you pay him?'

'First I asked for identification.'

'Did he show any?'

'Yes. His driver's licence.'

'A driver's licence made out to Andrew Leyden?'

'Yes.'

'Did the signature on the licence match those on the cheque?'

'Yes.'

'So you paid him.'

'Well, no, I called the main branch first.'

'Why'd you do that?'

'Because this was a cheque made out to cash, and the payer was also the endorser. So I wanted to make sure there

144

were sufficient funds in the account to cover the withdrawal.'

'And *were* there?'

'I was told there was a balance of $3,162.21 in Mr Leyden's account.'

'So did you then cash the cheque?'

'Yes, sir, I did.'

'Mr Graham, don't you read the newspapers?'

'I do.'

'Didn't you see anything about the Leyden murders?'

'Yes, I did. I'll tell you the truth, though, I never made a connexion. I mean, I *knew* the name Andrew Leyden, and I knew this cheque was signed and endorsed by Andrew Leyden, but it just never occurred to me they might be one and the same person. I'm sorry. It just never crossed my mind.'

'Thank you, Mr Graham,' Carella said.

Outside the bank, Kling said, 'So what do you think?'

'I think we now know why Damascus went back to the Leyden apartment Saturday.'

'Why?'

'To get Leyden's chequebook. Don't you remember Leyden's wire to the company? It asked his wife to send him a fresh chequebook and specifically mentioned it was in the top drawer of the dresser. Damascus must have known that too.'

'How *could* he have?'

'He was Rose Leyden's lover, wasn't he? The way this looks to me, he probably spent more time in *her* apartment than he did in his own. He must have had free run of the place whenever Leyden was on the road. So wouldn't he have been familiar with the contents of that dresser?'

'Then why didn't he grab the chequebook the night he killed them?'

'Because he panicked and ran.'

'But he *didn't* panic and run. He used Leyden's razor, remember?'

'Who says he used it that night? He was her *lover*, Bert,

in and out of that apartment constantly. He may have used the razor any number of times.'

'Yeah, but hold it just a second,' Kling said. 'If Damascus needed money, why didn't he go back to his *own* apartment where he'd left a perfectly good uncashed cheque from The Cozy Corners?'

'Because he knows we're looking for him. Besides, *that* cheque is only for a hundred and ten dollars and seventy-nine cents.'

'So? The one he cashed today isn't for a hell of a lot more.'

'The *first* one he cashed,' Carella said.

'You think there'll be more?'

'I think he'll milk the account dry before he takes off for wherever he's heading.'

'Then you think he killed them for the money? A measly three thousand bucks?'

'I know people who've killed people for a measly nickel,' Carella said, and nodded. 'My guess is that tomorrow morning bright and early, Damascus'll start hitting all the other branches of Commerce of America, cashing small cheques in each of them.' He nodded again, briefly. 'Only *this* time, we'll be ready for him.'

ELEVEN

THERE WERE seven branches of Commerce of America, but the police reasoned that Damascus would never try to pass himself off as Leyden at the branch where the dead man was known. They reasoned, too, that he would not try to cash a second cheque at the branch on Harris and Aley, and so that left only five banks to cover. There were sixteen detectives on the squad, two of them were on special assignment, three of whom were off duty, and three of whom were serving patrol days. That left eight available men; Lieutenant Byrnes took five of the eight, paired them off with patrolmen in plainclothes, and stationed them in the banks they guessed Damascus would hit.

Steve Carella was paired with Patrolman Benny Breach in the branch on Dock Street, all the way downtown in the financial section. The plan they had worked out with the bank officers was a simple one. If Damascus came up to any of the tellers with a cheque, the routine was not to vary an iota from what it had been yesterday when Edward Graham cashed the two-hundred-dollar cheque for him. The teller would first ask for identification, and then say he wanted to call the main branch to verify that there were sufficient funds in the account. He would then go to a telephone and dial the manager's office, where Carella and Breach would be waiting. Without arousing Damascus' suspicion in any way, he would smilingly come back to the window, ask him how he wanted the cash, and begin paying the cheque. By that time, Carella and Breach would have come out of the manager's office to make the arrest.

In practice, the plan worked almost that way.

Almost, but not quite.

Damascus came into the bank at 11.15 and walked directly

to one of the windows. He was a tall, good-looking man, well-dressed, exactly as Edward Graham had described him. He reached into his back pocket for his wallet, withdrew a cheque from it, and shoved it across the counter. His hands were huge. The printed names ROSE AND ANDREW LEYDEN fairly leaped up at the teller from the top of the cheque. He wet his lips, and then glanced at the cheque with only routine interest. It was made payable to Cash, in the amount of two hundred dollars; it was dated October 17th, and signed by Andrew Leyden. The teller turned it over, glanced at the endorsement on the back, and then casually said, 'May I see some identification, please, Mr Leyden?'

'Yes, certainly.' Damascus reached into his wallet. Locating the driver's licence, he smiled at the teller, and slid it across the counter.

'Thank you, sir,' the teller said, routinely comparing the signatures on the cheque with the one on the driver's licence. 'I'll just have to check our main branch, this won't take a moment.'

'Certainly.'

The teller walked away from his cage. He picked up a phone on the desk some ten feet from the window. When Carella answered, he said, 'He's here. Window number six.'

'Right,' Carella said, and hung up.

The teller nodded pleasantly, replaced the receiver on its cradle, smiled, and walked back to the window.

'How would you like that, Mr Leyden?' he asked.

'In tens, please.'

'Yes, sir.'

The teller opened the cash drawer. He took out a sheaf of tens, and began counting them off. He had reached seventy when Carella appeared at the window, gun in hand.

'Mr Damascus,' Carella said, 'you're under arrest.'

His answer was a short paralysing uppercut to the point of the jaw. His gun went off wildly, he heard footsteps clattering away across the marble floor and then Patrolman Breach's voice shouting, 'Stop or I'll shoot!' and then another gun going off. He stood dizzily swaying for a moment, heard Patrolman Breach firing again, shook his head to clear it, and then took aim on Damascus as he rushed towards the revolving entrance doors. He squeezed off the shot, saw the slug connect, saw blood on the neat grey shoulder of the suit, ran towards the revolving doors and was again surprised when Damascus reversed direction and kicked out at the gun in his hand. A woman screamed, the gun arced up into the air, spiralled down towards the marble floor, clattered away out of reach. Patrolman Breach was firing again, what did they teach you to *hit* at the Academy? Carella wondered, and then hurled himself on to Damascus' back as he moved again towards the revolving doors. The left sleeve of Damascus' jacket began to tear where Carella clung to it, finally ripped loose at the shoulder seam, and pulled free of the coat itself to expose a short-sleeved white shirt and a powerful forearm. Something on that forearm almost caused Carella to relax his grip. He opened his eyes wide in surprise and then, without stopping to think about the meaning of what he had just seen, he seized the ragged shoulder of the jacket with his right hand, pulled back on it, and hurled his left fist at the same instant. He felt nose bones splintering, heard a scream of outraged pain. He swung out again with his right, and then closed in for the kill, breathing harshly, swearing as he battered the big man to the marble floor of the bank, senseless.

On his left arm was a tattooed blue dagger with the name 'Andy' lettered across its blade in red.

In the squad room, in the presence of an attorney, Andrew Lloyd Leyden told them what had happened. He told them in his own words while Carella, Kling, Lieutenant Byrnes, and a police stenographer listened. His voice was very low as he spoke. He sat with his jacket draped over his bandaged shoulder, his head bent except when he glanced up at the detectives to ask rhetorical questions. They knew he was finished only when he stopped speaking; he gave no other

149

sign. The police stenographer typed the statement in triplicate, and they gave the original to Leyden to read before signing, while Byrnes studied one copy and Carella and Kling shared the other. The squad room was silent as the men read the confession:

I learned about them in May.

It was the beginning of May. I had been on the road, and when I came back I found out. I found out by accident. I didn't . . . you see . . . I didn't even know she was pregnant. You see, I had gone to the Coast in February, I take this one very long trip each spring, I leave here on February 1st, and I get back around May 1st, it's the longest trip I take each year. It . . . you see I had been gone since February and when . . . she miscarried, you see, and . . . and the doctor said the . . . he said she was . . . only two months pregnant so . . . so you see . . . I knew. I realized.

I didn't know what to do at first.

Whatever you do is wrong.

There's no <u>right</u> way for a man to behave when his wife and a stranger have made a fool of him, there's no way, all the ways are wrong. I kept wondering, you know, how she could have <u>done</u> it, didn't she know how much I <u>loved</u> her, I kept wondering that all the time. And I kept wondering, too, what would have happened if she <u>hadn't</u> miscarried. Was she planning to have the baby, did she think I was <u>that</u> great a fool, didn't she know I could count, for Christ's sake—or had they worked out something else? I didn't know, you see. I just didn't know. But there was nothing to do, nothing to do but shut up and carry the knowledge inside me. And die. Slowly die.

I . . . I had to find out who the man
was. I told her I had to go out of town for two
weeks, and instead I stayed here in the city and
watched the apartment, and saw him coming and
going just as if he _lived_ there with her. How
could she _do_ it, I wondered, how could she risk
so much, especially for such a . . . such a
person? I did a lot of checking, you see, I
followed him home, I found out his name, I
learned what kind of work he did—he was a
bouncer, you know—and the kind of . . . of
person he was. I couldn't understand how Rosie
could have had anything to do with him, he was
a . . . he was not a nice man. He had other
women, too, you know, at least two that I saw
him with in those weeks, God knows what filth he
was pouring into Rosie, what filth he had picked
up from those whores.

I guess . . .

I guess I was going to kill only him.

I followed him everywhere. I even took
a chance one night and went into The Cozy Corners, took a table near the back, where it was
dark—that was the night, yes, that was when I
found out he'd been 4-F. I was watching him,
you know, I watched every move he made, and
somebody, some guy drinking at the bar, just
casually said, 'Wally's a _big_ one, ain't he?'
and I just nodded, and he said, 'Never been in
the service, either, can you figure that? Big
husky guy like him?' I didn't pay much attention
to it then, I mean I didn't think it was strange
or anything because _I've_ never been in the service, either, you see, I had a punctured eardrum.
We're about the same size and build, Damascus
and me, and about the same age, that's another
thing I couldn't understand. I mean, if she

151

needed another man, if she absolutely had to do this, why'd she pick somebody who was like me?

I can't understand it at all.

I think by the time I bought the shotgun, I'd decided to kill them both. I wanted to shoot them in bed together, I wanted to kill them while they were doing it. The reason I bought a shotgun was that I wanted something that would do the most damage, inflict the greatest punishment. I think I'd seen a picture of a hunting accident in one of the men's magazines, I forget which one, and I guess that's when I realized what a gun could do to somebody's face. Especially a shotgun. Especially if you fired it close up. I just wanted to hurt them as much as they had hurt me, you see. I had no idea of getting away with it. I mean, I had no idea of destroying their faces so they couldn't be identified. I only thought of that later.

I thought of that when I was buying the shotgun. I didn't know you needed a permit to buy a shotgun in this city, but I found out soon enough. Then I learned I could go into the next state, right across the river, and buy a gun there without any trouble, so that's what I did. When the owner of the store asked me my name, I automatically said, 'Damascus,' and gave his address, and then when I was walking out—I bought the gun in Newfield, this was in August, before I left for the Coast again—while I was walking out of the shop, it occurred to me that Rosie had never been fingerprinted, and chances were Damascus hadn't either if he'd never been in the service. If I shot them both in the face, they wouldn't be recognized and their teeth would be gone and nobody could look up dental charts and maybe I could get away with it, kill them and actually get away with it. And then, I guess it was because I'd given Damascus' name when I bought the gun, the whole idea came to me, just like that. I would shoot them both, and I would let the police think Damascus was me. I was dead, anyway, wasn't I? Hadn't they both killed me by what they'd done? Okay, so I'd really kill off Andy Leyden, kill him once and for all, leave the city, maybe leave the country, start another life under another name while the police looked for my murderer.

The idea for the tattoo came to me on the plane to the Coast. A kid across the aisle was making a drawing with Magic Markers, and he got some of the ink on his fingers, and I thought how much the stain looked like tattooed skin, and I scouted around in L.A. for marking pens with thin points, and of course they make them in all sizes now, so that part was easy. I must have drawn this tattoo a hundred times until I got it just right. It's on my arm, you know, so all I had to do was look at it while I practiced drawing it over and over again. It's a simple tattoo, no fancy stuff, and it was easy to draw. I figured it would get by all right because it would be expected, do you see what I mean? The police would know that Andrew Leyden had a tattoo on his left arm, and when they looked at the body, they would find a tattoo right where it was supposed to be, so why would they even once stop to think it was fake? Did you think it was fake? Still, I was afraid that on the night I actually did it, I wouldn't have time to draw the tattoo on his arm, not after the noise of four shotgun blasts. But that was the horns of the dilemma, you see. I had to use

153

a shotgun in order to destroy their faces, but
I also had to put that fake tattoo on his arm so
everyone would think he was me. Did you think
he was me? Did everyone think he was me?

I wired the office from the Coast at nine
o'clock that Friday morning, and then called
Rosie to tell her to send me a fresh checkbook.
I really had run out of checkbooks, but that
wasn't why I'd called. I called to make certain
she was home and also to let her know I'd be out
there on the Coast while she was fooling around
with her boy friend here in the city. I caught
the 10:00 A.M. flight out of San Francisco and
arrived at International Airport here at 5:55
P.M. By six-thirty, I was in the city.

I didn't think I'd go through with it.

It was a long night, the longest night
in my life. I knew he worked until two o'clock,
you know, so I had to hang around until then, it
was a long wait. I had dinner about seven, and
then I walked around, and then I went to a
movie, and then I went into this bar and got
half-potted, and almost decided not to go ahead
with it. But I left there about one-thirty and
went to my building and waited downstairs for
him. He didn't show up until almost three-
thirty, I thought I'd missed him. I thought
maybe he'd got out of work early and I'd missed
him. But he showed up at last—a girl in a
yellow Buick dropped him off—and he went upstairs. I gave him enough time to take off his
clothes and get in bed with Rosie, and then
I took the shotgun out of the trunk of the car
where I'd left it from the day I bought it, and
I went up the stairs and let myself in the
kitchen door.

154

Rosie came into the living room and I shot her first.

When she fell I put another shot in her face.

I did the same to him.

In the bedroom.

Then I took off his jewelry, he was wearing a signet ring and an I.D. bracelet, and I put my wedding band on his left hand and my college ring on his other hand. Then I drew the tattoo on his arm.

I was very calm while I was drawing it. I thought sure the shots had been heard, they sounded so _loud_, you know?

But I was very calm.

When I finished the tattoo, it didn't look right. It looked too new and clean, it didn't look like the one I have on my arm. So I went around the apartment wiping my hand over any dusty surface I could find, deliberately getting my hand dirty, you see, and then I went back to where Damascus was lying on the floor and I rubbed the dirt onto the tattoo I'd drawn, to give it an older look, as if it had been there a long time, to take the _new_ look off it. Then I propped the gun in his hand. I guess I thought I'd make it look like a suicide.

That was an idea that just came to me while I was there.

I planned all the rest except that.

Lieutenant Byrnes put his copy of the confession on the desk and very softly said, 'All right, Mr Leyden, would you please sign all three copies?'

Leyden nodded. He took the pen Carella offered, turned the original copy so that he could sign it where a space had been left on the last page and then suddenly shook his head.

'What's the matter?' Byrnes asked.

155

'There's more,' Leyden said. 'I killed someone else.'

'What?' Byrnes said.

'I met a woman ... I ... when I was roaming around ... before ... before I went to the apartment. I met a woman in a bar and ... and later ... I ... I realized I'd ... I'd told her my name and ... and told her my wife was cheating on me. We were ... we were talking, you know, and I was upset, and I said too much. So ... I ... I ... after I did the others, I ... I went looking for her. I couldn't remember her name, you see, in all the excitement her name had gone out of my head, but I knew I had to find her to ... to make sure she ... So I went back to the bar, and the bartender wouldn't tell me what her name was, this must've been close to four o'clock in the morning, and I left there and was walking along wondering what to do when it came to me, all at once I remembered her name. I looked up her address in a phone book ...'

'What *was* her name, Mr Leyden?'

'Ryder. Marguerite Ryder.'

'Go on.'

'You getting this, Danny?' Carella asked the stenographer.

'Yo.'

'I went up there, and she said "Who is it?" and I said "This is the fellow you met in the bar", thinking if she didn't remember who I was I would leave her alone, there'd be no danger to me, do you understand? But she said "Mr Leyden?" and I said "Yes, Mr Leyden", and she opened the door and said "What is it?" I said I had to talk to her. She said it was very late, but I guess I looked desperate, she was a nice person, you see, she never once thought I would harm her. She was ... putting some dishes away or something, I don't even remember. We went straight into the kitchen, and the first thing I saw was a knife on the drainboard, and I picked it up and stabbed her without saying a word to her. I didn't want to but ... she knew my name, you see. She knew I was Andrew Leyden who was having trouble with his wife.'

156

The squad room was silent again.

'Danny, you want to get this new stuff typed?' Byrnes said.

'Yo,' the stenographer said.

Carella and Kling came down the squad-room steps with their topcoats open, the afternoon breeze coming in off the park across the street, carrying with it the late-autumn aroma of woodsmoke. The November sky behind the city's spires looked too uniform, a placid blue that had to be false, a backdrop created by scenic designers. Even the sounds of traffic were muted now that the frantic activity of the world's longest lunch hour had subsided; twilight seemed in gestation; the city already awaited the full onslaught of night.

They were both ravenously hungry. They had wanted to send out for sandwiches, so that they could finish the paperwork in the squad room, but Byrnes had insisted that they take a break. Now, in the waning sunlight of the afternoon, they felt the sudden chill of night, and quickened their pace, walking rapidly to the corner, turning it, and heading for the luncheonette in the middle of the block.

'Who's going to tell Meyer the Ryder case is closed?' Kling asked.

'We'd better break it gently,' Carella said.

'He'll have a coronary.'

'You know something?' Carella said. 'The fingerprints didn't even belong to him.'

'To who?'

'Damascus.'

'*What* fingerprints?'

'The ones on the razor, the ones on the shotgun, the ones all over the goddamn apartment. They were Leyden's all along.'

'Well, you can't blame the lab for that,' Kling said. 'They thought the dead man was Leyden. The wild prints . . .'

'I know, I was only saying. It can get pretty mixed up sometimes.'

'Yeah,' Kling said.

They walked silently and swiftly, their hands in their pockets. They were just outside the door to the luncheonette when Kling stopped and put his hand on Carella's arm, and earnestly said, 'Steve, would you have done it? If it had been Teddy with some guy, would you have done it?'

'No,' Carella answered.

ED McBAIN

'87th Precinct stories are outstanding . . . the feeling of crime in a big city, rough, sordid and in a queer way mechanical, comes through very well' THE SUNDAY TIMES.

EIGHTY MILLION EYES 25p
'Fast, exciting and realistic, well up to McBain's high standard' THE OBSERVER.

FUZZ 25p
'Splendid entertainment, engrossing, fast moving and often very funny' THE SUNDAY TIMES.

HE WHO HESITATES 25p
'Written with all the hard economy of the professional the story is gripping all the way' THE IRISH TIMES.

SHOTGUN 25p
'The best of today's lively inventive, convincing, suspenseful and wholly satisfactory' NEW YORK TIMES.

JOHN CREASEY

'There is no limit to his inventive genius in crime fiction.'
MANCHESTER EVENING NEWS.

'Handsome' West of the Yard:

TWO FOR INSPECTOR WEST 20p
SO YOUNG TO BURN 20p
INSPECTOR WEST REGRETS 20p
INSPECTOR WEST TAKES CHARGE 20p
ACCIDENT FOR INSPECTOR WEST 20p
A BEAUTY FOR INSPECTOR WEST 25p

'You can always rely on the phenomenal Creasey.'
OBSERVER.

A SELECTION OF POPULAR READING IN PAN

FICTION

ROYAL FLASH	George MacDonald Fraser	30p
THE FAME GAME	Rona Jaffe	40p
SILENCE ON MONTE SOLE	Jack Olsen	35p
A TASTE FOR DEATH	Peter O'Donnell	30p
TRAMP IN ARMOUR	Colin Forbes	30p
EMBASSY	Stephen Coulter	30p
AIRPORT	Arthur Hailey	37½p
HEIR TO FALCONHURST	Lance Horner	40p
REQUIEM FOR A WREN	Nevil Shute	30p
MADAME SERPENT	Jean Plaidy	30p
MURDER MOST ROYAL	Jean Plaidy	35p
CATHERINE	Juliette Benzoni	35p

NON-FICTION

THE SOMERSET & DORSET RAILWAY (illus.)	Robin Atthill	35p
THE WEST HIGHLAND RAILWAY (illus.)	John Thomas	35p
MY BEAVER COLONY (illus.)	Lars Wilsson	25p
THE SMALL GARDEN (illus.)	C. E. Lucas-Phillips	40p
HOW TO WIN CUSTOMERS	Heinz M. Goldmann	45p
THE NINE BAD SHOTS OF GOLF (illus.)	Jim Dante & Leo Diegel	35p

These and other advertised PAN Books are obtainable from all booksellers and newsagents. If you have any difficulty please send purchase price plus 5p postage to P.O. Box 11, Falmouth, Cornwall. While every effort is made to keep prices low, it is sometimes necessary to increase prices at short notice. PAN Books reserve the right to show new retail prices on covers which may differ from those advertised in the text or elsewhere.